Shadows 5

Shadows 5

Edited by
CHARLES L. GRANT

DOUBLEDAY & COMPANY, INC.
GARDEN CITY, NEW YORK
1982

Introduction copyright © 1982 by Charles L. Grant.
"The Gorgon" copyright © 1982 by Tanith Lee. By permission of the author.
"Stone Head" copyright © 1982 by Steve Rasnic Tem. By permission of the author.
"Pietà" copyright © 1982 by Alan Ryan. By permission of the author.
"Boxes" copyright © 1982 by Al Sarrantonio. By permission of the author.
"And I'll Be With You By and By" copyright © 1982 by Avon Swofford. By permission of the author.
"Dark Wings" copyright © 1982 by Phyllis Eisenstein. By permission of the author.
"Estrella" copyright © 1982 by Terry L. Parkinson. By permission of the author.
"Singles" copyright © 1982 by Marta Randall. By permission of the author.
"The Piano Man" copyright © 1982 by Beverly Evans. By permission of the author.
"Following the Way" copyright © 1982 by Alan Ryan. By permission of the author.
"Renewal" copyright © 1982 by Chelsea Quinn Yarbro. By permission of the author.

ISBN: 0-385-17756-9
Library of Congress Catalog Card Number 81-43740
Copyright © 1982 by Charles L. Grant
ALL RIGHTS RESERVED
PRINTED IN THE UNITED STATES OF AMERICA
FIRST EDITION

Contents

Introduction

In the five years since the birth of the *Shadows* series, a fair number of changes have taken place in the fantasy field: vampires have been supplanted by werewolves and like creatures both in print and on film, Tolkienesque High Fantasy has perhaps inevitably evolved away from its emphasis on dwarves, faeries, and elves toward a greater magical involvement with human characters, and there is the increasingly popular use of the label "Dark Fantasy" to mark those stories of horror and terror which contain, at the very least, a seductive hint of the supernatural. And the more it is used, the more it becomes exceedingly appropriate—not only does it serve to differentiate that material from High Fantasy, but it also implies that a great deal more is contained within the story than simply horror.

And in those stories which rise above the hackneyed, that is perfectly true.

From Robert Louis Stevenson to Peter Straub, Edgar Allan Poe to Stephen King, there has been and is a fascination with all things dark, with all things which inhabit the far side of midnight; and it is less the idea that there are *creatures* out there than it is the belief that those same *creatures* are not necessarily inexplicable, not completely beyond our comprehension. To cast light on black creates fields of grey in shades which do far more than show us what's out there; it also shows us that what's out there can just as easily be found in here—in our rooms, under our beds, in our closets . . . and in our minds.

And that which is in our minds is assuredly no less real than that which is concealed behind our favorite chair.

Sooner or later, then, most Dark Fantasy writers take a busman's holiday from those "things which go bump in the night" to attempt in their fiction an exploration of the mind's realm which lies *beyond* insanity. An aberration is, after all, just an aberration, and stories about characters who have lost their minds are stories of psychological terror, not fantasy. The fascination, then, lies not in the insanity itself but in the possibility that the insanity can be so powerful as to create a new segment of reality—not just for the afflicted character, but for the others who inhabit that character's world as well.

The creatures of the mind become the creatures that walk the streets, the alleyways, the woodland, the front porch.

No less real, no less deadly.

And because the writer, in attempting such material, faces difficulties of creation only hinted at in his usual work, the stories born of such labor, when they are successful, compare unquestionably favorably to anything written in any other genre.

This is not to say that Dark Fantasy is struggling to lay claim to the designations "Art" or "Serious Literature." To lay claim implies an outsider attempting to sneak in where he doesn't belong, or where he once was and from which he has been ousted by the so-called literary mavens. Dark Fantasy has never been on the outside. The best of it, as in the best of mainstream literature, sets real people disguised as fictional characters onto a plotted road to see what may be discovered through trial and/or triumph, discoveries not only about the characters themselves, but also about the readers, and all the rest of us.

Whether one meets windmills, psychoses, and/or Mr. Hyde along the way should be of less concern than what happens (in all senses of the word) when these crises complete their developments and the characters move on—one way or the other.

In that respect, "Dark" itself carries with it much more weight than simply midnight.

And "Fantasy," like a shadow, is not always what we think it is.

Charles L. Grant
Budd Lake, New Jersey
1981

Shadows 5

Introduction

Tanith Lee, winner of the British Fantasy Award for her novel
Sabella, *has written numerous children's books, radio and televi-*
sion plays, sf and fantasy novels, all with a dedication and fervor
which puts many of her colleagues to shame. She is meticulous
about her work, demanding much both of herself and her readers.
She also understands better than most that shadows of the soul are
just as terrifying as shadows on the wall.

THE GORGON

by Tanith Lee

The small island, which lay off the larger island of Daphaeu, obviously contained a secret of some sort, and, day by day, and partic-
ularly night by night, began to exert an influence on me, so that I
must find it out.

Daphaeu itself (or more correctly herself, for she was a female
country, voluptuous and cruel by turns in the true antique fashion
of the Goddess) was hardly enormous. A couple of roads, a tangle
of sheep tracks, a precarious, escalating village, rocks and hillsides
thatched by blistered grass. All of which overhung an extraordinary sea, unlike any sea which I have encountered elsewhere in
Greece. Water which might be mistaken for blueness from a distance, but which, from the harbor or the multitude of caves and
coves that undermined the island, revealed itself a clear and suc-
culent green, like milky limes or the bottle glass of certain spirits.

On my first morning, having come on to the natural terrace (the
only recommendation of the hovel-like accommodation) to look
over this strange green ocean, I saw the smaller island, lying like a
little boat of land moored just wide of Daphaeu's three hills. The
day was clear, the water frilled with white where it hit the fangs in
the interstices below the terrace. About the smaller island, barely

a ruffle showed. It seemed to glide up from the sea, smooth as mirror. The little island was verdant, also. Unlike Daphaeu's limited stands of stone pine, cypress, and cedar, the smaller sister was clouded by a still, lambent haze of foliage that looked to be woods. Visions of groves, springs, a ruined temple, a statue of Pan playing the panpipes forever in some glade—where only yesterday, it might seem, a thin column of aromatic smoke had gone up—these images were enough, fancifully, to draw me into inquiries about how the small island might be reached. And when my inquiries met first with a polite bevy of excuses, next with a refusal, last with a blank wall of silence, as if whoever I mentioned the little island to had gone temporarily deaf or mad, I became, of course, insatiable to get to it, to find out what odd superstitious thing kept these people away. Naturally, the Daphaeui were not friendly to me at any time beyond the false friendship one anticipates extended to a man of another nationality and clime, who can be relied on to pay his bills, perhaps allow himself to be overcharged, even made a downright monkey of in order to preserve goodwill. In the normal run of things, I could have had anything I wanted in exchange for a pack of local lies, a broad local smile, and a broader local price. That I could not get to the little island puzzled me. I tried money and I tried barter. I even, in a reckless moment, probably knowing I would not succeed, offered Pitos, one of the younger fishermen, the gold and onyx ring he coveted. My sister had made it for me, the faithful copy of an intaglio belonging to the House of Borgia, no less. Generally, Pitos could not pass the time of day with me without mentioning the ring, adding something in the nature of: "If ever you want a great service, any great service, I will do it for that ring." I half believe he would have stolen or murdered for it, certainly shared the bed with me. But he would not, apparently, even for the Borgia ring, take me to the little island.

"You think too much of foolish things," he said to me. "For a big writer, that is not good."

I ignored the humorous aspect of "big," equally inappropriate in the sense of height, girth, or fame. Pitos's English was fine, and when he slipped into mild inaccuracies, it was likely to be a decoy.

"You're wrong, Pitos. That island has a story in it somewhere. I'd take a bet on it."

"No fish today," said Pitos. "Why you think that is?"

I refrained from inventively telling him I had seen giant swordfish leaping from the shallows by the smaller island.

I found I was prowling Daphaeu, but only on the one side, the side where I would get a view—or views—of her sister. I would climb down into the welter of coves and smashed emerald water to look across at her. I would climb up and stand, leaning on the sunblasted walls of a crumbling church, and look at the small island. At night, crouched over a bottle of wine, a scatter of manuscript, moths falling like rain in the oil lamp, my stare stayed fixed on the small island, which, as the moon came up, would seem turned to silver or to some older metal, Nemean metal perhaps, sloughed from the moon herself.

Curiosity accounts for much of this, and contrasuggestiveness. But the influence I presently began to feel, that I cannot account for exactly. Maybe it was only the writer's desire to fantasize rather than to work. But each time I reached for the manuscript I would experience a sort of distraction, a sort of calling—uncanny, poignant, like nostalgia, though for a place I had never visited.

I am very bad at recollecting my dreams, but one or twice, just before sunrise, I had a suspicion I had dreamed of the island. Of walking there, hearing its inner waters, the leaves brushing my hands and face.

Two weeks went by, and precious little had been done in the line of work. And I had come to Daphaeu with the sole intention of working. The year before, I had accomplished so much in a month of similar islands—or had they been similar?—that I had looked for results of some magnitude. In all of fourteen days I must have squeezed out two thousand words, and most of those dreary enough that the only covers they would ever get between would be those of the trash can. And yet it was not that I could not produce work, it was that I knew, with blind and damnable certainty, that the work I needed to be doing sprang from that spoonful of island.

The first day of the third week I had been swimming in the calm stretch of sea west of the harbor and had emerged to sun myself and smoke on the parched hot shore. Presently Pitos appeared, having scented my cigarettes. Surgical and government health warnings have not yet penetrated to spots like Daphaeu, where filtered tobacco continues to symbolize Hollywood or some other amorphous, anacronistic surrealism still hankered after and long vanished from the real world beyond. Once Pitos had acquired his cigarette, he sprawled down on the dry grass, grinned, indicated the Borgia ring, and mentioned a beautiful cousin of his, whether male or female I cannot be sure. After this had been cleared out of the way, I said to him, "You know how the currents run. I was thinking of a slightly more adventurous swim. But I'd like your advice."

Pitos glanced at me warily. I had had the plan as I lazed in the velvet water. Pitos was already starting to guess it.

"Currents are very dangerous. Not to be trusted, except by harbor."

"How about between Daphaeu and the other island? It can't be more than a quarter mile. The sea looks smooth enough, once you break away from the shoreline here."

"No," said Pitos. I waited for him to say there were no fish, or a lot of fish, or that his brother had gotten a broken thumb, or something of the sort. But Pitos did not resort to this. Troubled and angry, he stabbed my cigarette, half-smoked, into the turf. "Why do you want to go to the island so much?"

"Why does nobody else want me to go there?"

He looked up then, and into my eyes. His own were very black, sensuous, carnal earthbound eyes, full of orthodox sins, and extremely young in a sense that had nothing to do with physical age, but with race, I suppose, the youngness of ancient things, like Pan himself, quite possibly.

"Well," I said at last, "are you going to tell me or not? Because believe me, I intend to swim over there today or tomorrow."

"No," he said again. And then: "You should not go. On the island there is a . . ." and he said a word in some tongue neither Greek nor Turkish, not even the corrupt Spanish that sometimes peregrinates from Malta.

"A *what*?"

Pitos shrugged helplessly. He gazed out to sea, a safe sea without islands. He seemed to be putting something together in his mind and I let him do it, very curious now, pleasantly unnerved by this waft of the occult I had already suspected to be the root cause of the ban.

Eventually he turned back to me, treated me once more to the primordial innocence of his stare, and announced:

"The cunning one."

"Ah," I said. Both irked and amused, I found myself smiling. At this, Pitos's face grew savage with pure rage, an expression I had never witnessed before—the façade kept for foreigners had well and truly come down.

"Pitos," I said, "I don't understand."

"*Meda,*" he said then, the Greek word, old Greek.

"Wait," I said. I caught at the name, which was wrong, trying to fit it to a memory. Then the list came back to me, actually from Graves, the names which meant "the cunning": Meda, Medea, Medusa.

"Oh," I said. I hardly wanted to offend him further by bursting into loud mirth. At the same time, even while I was trying not to laugh, I was aware of the hair standing up on my scalp and neck. "You're telling me there is a gorgon on the island."

Pitos grumbled unintelligibly, stabbing the dead cigarette over and over into the ground.

"I'm sorry, Pitos, but it can't be Medusa. Someone cut her head off quite a few years ago. A guy called Perseus."

His face erupted into that awful expression again, mouth in a rictus, tongue starting to protrude, eyes flaring at me—quite abruptly I realized he wasn't raging, but imitating the visual panic-contortions of a man turning inexorably to stone. Since that is what the gorgon is credited with, literally petrifying men by the sheer horror of her countenance, it now seemed almost pragmatic of Pitos to be demonstrating. It was, too, a creditable facsimile of the sculpted gorgon's face sometimes used to seal ovens and jars. I wondered where he had seen one to copy it so well.

"All right," I said. "OK, Pitos, fine." I fished in my shirt, which was lying on the ground, and took out some money to give him, but he recoiled. "I'm sorry," I said, "I don't think it merits the ring. Unless you'd care to row me over there after all."

The boy rose. He looked at me with utter contempt, and without another word, before striding off up the shore. The mashed cigarette protruded from the grass and I lay and watched it, the tiny strands of tobacco slowly crisping in the heat of the sun, as I plotted my route from Daphaeu.

Dawn seemed an amiable hour. No one in particular about on that side of the island, the water chill but flushing quickly with warmth as the sun reached over it. And the tide in the right place to navigate the rocks. . . .

Yes, dawn would be an excellent time to swim out to the gorgon's island.

The gods were on my side, I concluded as I eased myself into the open sea the following morning. Getting clear of the rocks was no problem, their channels only half filled by the returning tide. While just beyond Daphaeu's coast I picked up one of those contrary currents that lace the island's edges and which, tide or no, would funnel me away from shore.

The swim was ideal, the sea limpid and no longer any more than cool. Sunlight filled in the waves and touched Daphaeu's retreating face with gold. Barely altered in thousands of years, either rock or sea or sun. And yet one knew that against all the claims of romantic fiction, this place did not look now as once it had. Some element in the air or in time itself changes things. A young man of the Bronze Age, falling asleep at sunset in his own era, waking at sunrise in mine, looking about him, would not have known where he was. I would swear to that.

Such thoughts I had leisure for in my facile swim across to the wooded island moored off Daphaeu.

As I had detected, the approach was smooth, virtually inviting. I cruised in as if sliding along butter. A rowboat would have had no more difficulty. The shallows were clear, empty of rocks, and, if anything, greener than the water off Daphaeu.

I had not looked much at Medusa's Island (I had begun jokingly to call it this) as I crossed, knowing I would have all the space on my arrival. So I found myself wading in on a seamless beach of rare glycerine sand and, looking up, saw the mass of trees spilling from the sky.

The effect was incredibly lush—so much heavy green, and seemingly quite impenetrable, while the sun struck in glistening shafts, lodging like arrows in the foliage, which reminded me very intensely of huge clusters of grapes on a vine. Anything might lie behind such a barricade.

It was already beginning to get hot. Dry, I put on the loose cotton shirt and ate breakfast packed in the same waterproof wrapper, standing on the beach impatient to get on.

As I moved forward, a bird shrilled somewhere in its cage of boughs, sounding an alarm of invasion. But surely the birds, too, would be stone on Medusa's Island, if the legends were correct. And when I stumbled across the remarkable stone carving of a man in the forest, I would pause in shocked amazement at its verisimilitude to life. . . .

Five minutes into the thickets of the wood, I did indeed stumble on a carving, but it was of a moss-grown little faun. My pleasure in the discovery was considerably lessened, however, when investigation told me it was scarcely classical in origin. Circa 1920 would be nearer the mark.

A further minute and I had put the faun from my mind. The riot of waterfalling plants through which I had been picking my way broke open suddenly on an inner vista much wider than I had anticipated. While the focal point of the vista threw me completely, I cannot say what I had really been expecting. The grey-white stalks of pillars, some temple shrine, the spring with its votary of greenish rotted bronze, none of these would have surprised me. On the other hand, to find a house before me took me completely by surprise. I stood and looked at it in abject dismay, cursing its wretched normality until I gradually began to see the house was not normal in the accepted sense.

It had been erected probably at the turn of the century, when such things were done. An eccentric two-storied building, intransigently European—that is, the Europe of the north—with its dark walls and arched roofing. Long windows, smothered by the proximity of the wood, received and refracted no light. The one unique and startling feature—startling because of its beauty—was the parade of columns that ran along the terrace, in form and choreography for all the world like the columns of Knossos, differing only in color. For these stems of the gloomy house were of a luminous sea-green marble, and shone as the windows did not.

Before the house was a stretch of rough-cut lawn, tamarisk, and one lost dying olive tree. As I was staring, an apparition seemed to manifest out of the center of the tree. For a second we peered at each other before he came from the bushes with a clashing of gnarled brown forearms. He might have been an elderly satyr; I, patently, was only a swimmer, with my pale foreigner's tan, my bathing trunks, the loose shirt. It occurred to me at last that I was conceivably trespassing. I wished my Greek were better.

He planted himself before me and shouted intolerantly, and anyone's Greek was good enough to get his drift. "Go! Go!" He was ranting, and he began to wave a knife with which, presumably, he had been pruning or mutilating something. "Go. You *go!*"

I said I had been unaware anybody lived on the island. He took no notice. He went on waving the knife and his attitude provoked me. I told him sternly to put the knife down, that I would leave when I was ready, that I had seen no notice to the effect that the island was private property. Generally I would never take a chance like this with someone so obviously qualified to be a luna-tic, but my position was so vulnerable, so ludicrous, so entirely in-defensible, that I felt bound to act firmly. Besides which, having reached the magic grotto and found it was not as I had visualized, I was still very reluctant to abscond with only a memory of dark windows and sea-green columns to brood upon.

The maniac was by now quite literally foaming, due most likely to a shortage of teeth, but the effect was alarming, not to mention unaesthetic. As I was deciding which fresh course to take and if there might be one, a woman's figure came out on to the terrace. I had the impression of a white frock, before an odd, muffled voice called out a rapid—too rapid for my translation—stream of pecu-liarly accented Greek. The old man swung around, gazed at the figure, raised his arms, and bawled another foaming torrent to the effect that I was a bandit or some other kind of malcontent. While he did so, agitated as I was becoming, I nevertheless took in what I could of the woman standing between the columns. She was mostly in shadow, just the faded white dress with a white scarf at the neck marking her position. And then there was an abrupt flash of warmer pallor that was her hair. A blond Greek, or maybe just a peroxided Greek. At any rate, no snakes.

The drama went on, from his side, from hers. I finally got tired of it, went by him, and walked toward the terrace, pondering, rather too late, if I might not be awarded the knife in my back. But almost as soon as I started to move, she leaned forward a little and she called another phrase to him, which this time I made out, telling him to let me come on.

When I reached the foot of the steps, I halted, really involuntarily, struck by something strange about her. Just as the strangeness of the house had begun to strike me, not its evident strangeness, the ill-marriage to location, the green pillars, but a strangeness of atmosphere, items the unconscious eye notices, where the physical eye is blind and will not explain. And so with her. What was it? Still in shadow, I had the impression she might be in her early thirties, from her figure, her movements, but she had turned away as I approached, adjusting some papers on a wicker table.

"Excuse me," I said. I stopped and spoke in English. For some reason I guessed she would be familiar with the language, perhaps only since it was current on Daphaeu. "Excuse me. I had no idea the island was private. No one gave me the slightest hint—"

"You are English," she broke in, in the vernacular, proving the guess to be correct.

"Near enough. I find it easier to handle than Greek, I confess."

"Your Greek is very good," she said with the indifferent patronage of one who is multilingual. I stood there under the steps, already fascinated. Her voice was the weirdest I had ever heard, muffled, almost unattractive, and with the most incredible accent, not Greek at all. The nearest approximation I could come up with was Russian, but I could not be sure.

"Well," I said. I glanced over my shoulder and registered that the frothy satyr had retired into his shrubbery; the knife glinted as it slashed tamarisk in lieu of me. "Well, I suppose I should retreat to Daphaeu. Or am I permitted to stay?"

"Go, stay," she said. "I do not care at all."

She turned then, abruptly, and my heart slammed into the base of my throat. A childish silly reaction, yet I was quite unnerved, for now I saw what it was that had seemed vaguely peculiar from a distance. The lady on Medusa's Island was masked.

She remained totally still and let me have my reaction, neither helping nor hindering me.

It was an unusual mask, or usual—I am unfamiliar with the norm of such things. It was made of some matt-light substance that toned well with the skin of her arms and hands, possibly not so well with that of her neck, where the scarf provided camouflage. Besides which, the chin of the mask—this certainly an extra to any mask I had ever seen—continued under her own. The mask's physiognomy was bland, nondescriptly pretty in a way that was somehow grossly insulting to her. Before confronting the mask, if I had tried to judge the sort of face she would have, I would have suspected a coarse, rather heavy beauty, probably redeemed by one chiseled feature—a small slender nose, perhaps. The mask, however, was vacuous. It did not suit her, was not true to her. Even after three minutes I could tell as much, or thought I could, which amounts to the same thing.

The blond hair, seeming natural as the mask was not, cascaded down, lush as the foliage of the island. A blond Greek, then, like the golden Greeks of Homer's time, when gods walked the earth in disguise.

In the end, without any help or hindrance from her, as I have said, I pulled myself together. As she had mentioned no aspect of her state, neither did I. I simply repeated what I had said before: "Am I permitted to stay?"

The mask went on looking at me. The astonishing voice said: "You wish to stay so much. What do you mean to do here?"

Talk to you, oblique lady, and wonder what lies behind the painted veil.

"Look at the island, if you'll let me. I found the statue of a faun near the beach." Elaboration implied I should lie: "Someone told me there was an old shrine here."

"Ah!" She barked. It was apparently a laugh. "No one," she said, "*told* you anything about this place."

I was at a loss. Did she know what was said? "Frankly, then, I romantically hoped there might be."

"Unromantically, there is not. No shrine. No temple. My father bought the faun in a shop in Athens. A tourist shop. He had vulgar tastes but he knew it, and that has a certain charm, does it not?"

"Yes, I suppose it does. Your father—"

She cut me short again.

"The woods cover all the island. Except for an area behind the house. We grow things there, and we keep goats and chickens. We are very domesticated. Very sufficient for ourselves. There is a spring of fresh water, but no votary. No *genius loci*. I am *so* sorry to dash your dreams to pieces."

It suggested itself to me, from her tone of amusement, from little inflections that were coming and going in her shoulders now, that she might be enjoying this, enjoying, if you like, putting me down as an idiot. Presumably visitors were rare. Perhaps it was even fun for her to talk to a man, youngish and unknown, though admittedly never likely to qualify for anyone's centerfold.

"But you have no objections to my being here," I pursued. "And your father?"

"My parents are dead," she informed me. "When I employed the plural, I referred to him," she gestured with a broad sweep of her hand to the monster on the lawn, "and a woman who attends to the house. My servants, my unpaid servants. I have no money anymore. Do you see this dress? It is my mother's dress. How lucky I am the same fitting as my mother, do you not think?"

"Yes. . . ."

I was put in mind, suddenly, of myself as an ambassador at the court of some notorious female potentate, Cleopatra, say, or Catherine de Medici.

"You are very polite," she said as if telepathically privy to my fantasies.

"I have every reason to be."

"What reason?"

"I'm trespassing. You treat me like a guest."

"And how," she said, vainglorious all at once, "do you rate my English?"

"It's wonderful."

"I speak eleven languages fluently," she said with offhanded boastfulness. "Three more I can read very well."

I liked her. This display, touching and magnificent at once, her angular theatrical gesturings, which now came more and more often, her hair, her flat-waisted figure in its 1940s dress, her large well-made hands, and her challenging me with the mask, saying nothing to explain it, all this hypnotized me.

I said something to express admiration and she barked again, throwing back her blond head and irresistibly, though only for a moment, conjuring Garbo's Queen Christina.

Then she walked down the steps straight to me, demonstrating something else I had deduced, that she was only about an inch shorter than I.

"I," she said, "will show you the island. Come."

She showed me the island. Unsurprisingly, it was small. To go directly around it would maybe have taken less than thirty minutes. But we lingered, over a particular tree, a view, and once we sat down on the ground near the gushing milk-white spring. The basin under the spring, she informed me, had been added in 1910. A little bronze nymph presided over the spot, dating from the same year, which you could tell in any case from the way her classical costume and her filleted hair had been adapted to the fashions of hobble skirt and Edwardian coiffeur. Each age imposes its own overlay on the past.

Behind the house was a scatter of the meager white dwellings that make up such places as the village on Daphaeu, now plainly unoccupied and put to other uses. Sheltered from the sun by a colossal cypress, six goats played about in the grass. Chickens and an assortment of other fowl strutted up and down, while a pig—or pigs—grunted somewhere out of sight. Things grew in strips and patches, and fruit trees and vines ended the miniature plantation before the woods resumed. Self-sufficiency of a tolerable kind, I supposed. But there seemed, from what she said, no contact maintained with any other area, as if the world did not exist. Postulate that a blight or harsh weather intervened, what then? And the old satyr, how long would he last to tend the plots? He looked two hundred now, which on the islands probably meant sixty. I did not ask her what contingency plans she had for these emergencies and inevitabilities. What good, after all, are most plans? We could be invaded from Andromeda tomorrow, and what help for us all then? Either it is in your nature to survive—somehow, anyhow—or it is not.

She had well and truly hooked me, of course. If I had met her in Athens, some sun-baked afternoon, I would have felt decidedly out of my depth, taken her for cocktails, and foundered before we had even reached the dinner hour. But here, in this pulsing green bubble of light and leaves straight out of one's most irrational visions of the glades of Arcadia, conversation, however erratic, communication, however eccentric, was happening. The most inexplicable thing of all was that the mask had ceased almost immediately to bother me. I cannot, as I look back, properly account for this, for to spend a morning, a noon, an afternoon, allowing yourself to become fundamentally engaged by a woman whose face you have not seen, whose face you are actively being prevented from seeing, seems now incongruous to the point of perversity. But there it is. We discussed Ibsen, Dickens, Euripides, and Jung. I remembered trawling anecdotes of a grandfather, mentioned my sister's jewelry store in St. Louis, listened to an astonishing description of wild birds flying in across a desert from a sea. I assisted her over rocky turf, flirted with her, felt excited by and familiar with her, all this with her masked face before me. As if the mask, rather than being a part of her, meant no more than the frock she had elected to wear or the narrow-heeled vanilla shoes she had chosen to put on. As if I knew her face totally and had no need to be shown it, the face of her movements and her ridiculous voice.

But in fact, I could not even make out her eyes, only the shine in them when they caught the light, flecks of luminescence but not color, for the eyeholes of the mask were long-lidded and rather small. I must have noticed, too, that there was no aperture in the lips, and this may have informed me that the mask must be removed for purposes of eating or drinking. I really do not know. I can neither excuse nor quite understand myself, seen in the distance there with her on her island. Hartley tells us that the past is another country. Perhaps we also were other people—strangers—yesterday. But when I think of this, I remember, too, the sense of drawing I had had, of being magnetized to that shore, those trees, the nostalgia for a place I had never been to. For she, it may be true to say, was a figment of that nostalgia, as if I had known her and come back to her. Some enchantment, then. Not Medusa's Island, but Circe's.

The afternoon, even through the dapple *L'Après-midi d'un Faune* effect of the leaves, was a viridian furnace when we regained the house. I sat in one of the wicker chairs on the terrace and woke with a start of embarrassment to hear her laughing at me.

"You are tired and hungry. I must go into the house for a while. I will send Kleia to you with some wine and food."

It made a bleary sense, and when I woke again it was to find an old fat woman in the ubiquitous Grecian island black—demonstrably Kleia—setting down a tray of pale red wine, amber cheese, and dark bread.

"Where is—" I realized I did not know the enchantress's name.

In any event, the woman only shook her head, saying brusquely in Greek: "No English. No English."

And when I attempted to ask again in Greek where my hostess had gone, Kleia waddled away, leaving me unanswered. So I ate the food, which was passable, and drank the wine, which was very good, imagining her faun-buying father putting down an enormous patrician cellar, then fell asleep again, sprawled in the chair.

When I awoke, the sun was setting and the clearing was swimming in red light and rusty violet shadows. The columns burned as if they were internally on fire, holding the core of the sunset, it appeared, some while after the sky had cooled and the stars became visible, a trick of architectural positioning that won my awe and envy. I was making a mental note to ask her who had been responsible for the columns, and jumped when she spoke to me, softly and hoarsely, almost seductively, from just behind my chair —thereby promptly making me forget to ask any such thing.

"Come into the house now. We will dine soon."

I got up, saying something lame about imposing on her, though we were far beyond that stage.

"Always," she said to me, "you apologize. There is no imposition. You will be gone tomorrow."

How do you know? I nearly inquired, but prevented myself. What guarantee? Even if the magic food did not change me into a swine, perhaps my poisoned dead body would be carried from the feast and cast into the sea, gone, well and truly, to Poseidon's fishes. You see, I did not trust her, even though I was somewhat in love with her. The element of her danger—for she *was* dangerous in some obscure way—may well have contributed to her attraction.

We went into the house, which in itself alerted me. I had forgotten the great curiosity I had had to look inside it. There was a shadowy, unlit entrance hall, a sort of Roman atrium of a thing. Then we passed, she leading, into a small salon that took my breath away. It was lined all over—floor, ceiling, walls—with the sea-green marble the columns were made of. Whether in good taste or bad I am not qualified to say, but the effect, instantaneous and utter, was of being beneath the sea. Smoky oil lamps of a very beautiful Art Nouveau design hung from the profundity of the green ceiling, lighting the dreamlike swirls and oceanic variations of the marble so they seemed to breathe, definitely to move, like nothing else but waves. Shoes on that floor would have squeaked or clattered unbearably, but I was barefoot and so now was she.

A mahogany table with a modest placing for eight stood centrally. Only one place was laid.

I looked at it and she said, "I do not dine, but that will not prevent you."

An order. I considered vampires idly, but mainly I was subject to an infantile annoyance. Without quite realizing it, I had looked for the subtraction of the mask when she ate and now this made me very conscious of the mask for the first time since I had originally seen it.

We seated ourselves, she two places away from me. And I began to feel nervous. To eat this meal while she watched me did not appeal. And now the idea of the mask, unconsidered all morning, all afternoon, stole over me like an incoming tide.

Inevitably, I had not dressed for dinner, having no means, but she had changed her clothes and was now wearing a high-collared, long, grey gown, her mother's again, no doubt. It had the fragile look of age, but was very feminine and appealing for all that. Above it, the mask now reared, stuck out like the proverbial sore thumb.

The mask. What on earth was I going to do, leered at by that myopic, soulless face which had suddenly assumed such disastrous importance?

Kleia waddled in with the dishes. I cannot recall the meal, save that it was spicy and mostly vegetable. The wine came too, and I drank it. And as I drank the wine, I began to consider seriously, for the first time (which seems very curious indeed to me now) the reason for the mask. What did it hide? A scar, a birthmark? I drank her wine and I saw myself snatch off the mask, take in the disfigurement, unquelled, and behold the painful gratitude in her eyes as she watched me. I would inform her of the genius of surgeons. She would repeat she had no money. I would promise to pay for the operation.

Suddenly she startled me by saying: "Do you believe that we have lived before?"

I looked in my glass, that fount of wisdom and possibility, and said, "It seems as sensible a proposition as any of the others I've ever heard."

I fancied she smiled to herself and do not know why I thought that; I know now I was wrong.

Her accent had thickened and distorted further when she said, "I rather hope that I have lived before. I could wish to think I may live again."

"To compensate for this life?" I said brutishly. I had not needed to be so obvious when already I had been given the implication on a salver.

"Yes. To compensate for this."

I downed all the wisdom and possibility left in my glass, swallowed an extra couple of times, and said, "Are you going to tell me why you wear a mask?"

As soon as I had said it, I grasped that I was drunk. Nor was it a pleasant drunkenness. I did not like the demanding tone I had taken with her, but I was angry at having allowed the game to go on for so long. I had no knowledge of the rules, or pretended I had not. And I could not stop myself. When she did not reply, I added on a note of ghastly banter, "Or shall I guess?"

She was still, seeming very composed. Had this scene been enacted before? Finally she said, "I would suppose you do guess it is to conceal something that I wear it."

"Something you imagine worth concealing, which, perhaps, isn't."

That was the stilted fanfare of bravado. I had braced myself, flushed with such stupid confidence.

"Why not," I said, and I grow cold when I remember how I spoke to her, "take the damn thing off. Take off the mask and drink a glass of wine with me."

A pause. Then, "No," she said.

Her voice was level and calm. There was neither eagerness nor fear in it.

"Go on," I said, the drunk not getting his way, aware (oh God) he could get it by the power of his intention alone, "please. You're an astounding woman. You're like this island. A fascinating mystery. But I've seen the island. Let me see you."

"No," she said.

I started to feel, even through the wine, that I had made an indecent suggestion to her, and this, along with the awful clichés I was bringing out, increased my anger and my discomfort.

"For heaven's sake," I said, "do you know what they call you on Daphaeu?"

"Yes."

"This is absurd. You're frightened—"

"No. I am not afraid."

"Afraid. Afraid to let me see. But maybe I can help you."

"No. You cannot help me."

"How can you be sure?"

She turned in her chair, and all the way to face me with the mask. Behind her, everywhere about her, the green marble dazzled.

"If you know," she said, "what I am called on Daphaeu, are you not uneasy as to what you may see?"

"Jesus. Mythology and superstition and ignorance. I assure you, I won't turn to stone."

"It is I," she said quietly, "who have done that."

Something about the phrase, the way in which she said it, chilled me. I put down my glass and, in that instant, her hands went to the sides of the mask and her fingers worked at some complicated strap arrangement which her hair had covered.

"Good," I said, "good. I'm glad—"

But I faltered over it. The cold night sea seemed to fill my veins where the warm red wine had been. I had been heroic and sure and bold, the stuff of celluloid. But now that I had my way, with hardly any preliminary, what *would* I see? And then she drew the plastic away and I saw.

I sat there, and then I stood up. The reflex was violent, and the chair scraped over the marble with an unbearable noise. There are occasions, though rare, when the human mind grows blank of all thought. I had no thought as I looked at her. Even now, I can evoke those long, long, empty seconds, that lapse of time. I recollect only the briefest confusion, when I believed she still played some kind of hideous game, that what I witnessed was a product of her decision and her will, a gesture—

After all, Pitos had done this very thing to illustrate and endorse his argument, produced this very expression, the eyes bursting from the head, the jaw rigidly outthrust, the tendons in the neck straining, the mouth in the grimace of a frozen, agonized scream, the teeth visible, the tongue slightly protruding. The gorgon's face on the jar or the oven. The face so ugly, so demented, so terrible, it could petrify.

The awful mouth writhed.

"You have seen," she said. Somehow the stretched and distorted lips brought out these words. There was even that nuance of humor I had heard before, the smile, although physically a smile would have been out of the question. "You have seen."

She picked up the mask again, gently, and put it on, easing the underpart of the plastic beneath her chin to hide the convulsed tendons in her throat. I stood there, motionless. Childishly I informed myself that now I comprehended the reason for her peculiar accent, which was caused, not by some exotic foreign extraction, but by the atrocious malformation of jaw, tongue, and lips, which somehow must be fought against for every sound she made.

I went on standing there, and now the mask was back in place.

"When I was very young," she said, "I suffered, without warning, from a form of fit or stroke. Various nerve centers were paralyzed. My father took me to the very best of surgeons, you may comfort yourself with that. Unfortunately, any effort to correct the damage entailed a penetration of my brain so uncompromisingly delicate that it was reckoned impossible, for it would surely render me an idiot. Since my senses, faculties, and intelligence were otherwise unaffected, it was decided not to risk this dire surgery, and my doctors resorted instead to alternative therapies, which, patently, were unsuccessful. As the months passed, my body adjusted to the unnatural physical tensions resulting from my facial paralysis. The pain of the rictus faded, or grew acceptable. I learned both how to eat, and how to converse, although the former activity is not attractive and I attend to it in private. The mask was made for me in Athens. I am quite fond of it. The man who designed it had worked a great many years in the theatre and could have made me a face of enormous beauty or character, but this seemed pointless, even wasteful."

There was a silence, and I realized her explanation was finished.

Not once had she stumbled. There was neither hurt nor madness in her inflection. There *was* something . . . at the time I missed it, though it came to me after. Then I knew only that she was far beyond my pity or my anguish, far away indeed from my terror.

"And now," she said, rising gracefully, "I will leave you to eat your meal in peace. Good night."

I wanted, or rather I felt impelled, to stay her with actions or sentences, but I was incapable of either. She walked out of the green marble room and left me there. It is a fact that for a considerable space of time I did not move.

I did not engage the swim back to Daphaeu that night; I judged myself too drunk and slept on the beach at the edge of the trees, where at sunrise the tidal water woke me with a strange low hissing. Green sea, green sunlight through leaves. I swam away and found my course through the warming ocean and fetched up, exhausted and swearing, bruising myself on Daphaeu's fangs that had not harmed me when I left her. I did not see Pitos anywhere about, and that evening I caught the boat which would take me to the mainland.

There is a curious thing which can happen with human beings.

It is the ability to perform for days or weeks like balanced and
cheerful automata, when some substrata, something upon which
our codes or our hopes had firmly rested, has given way. Men who
lose their wives or their God are quite capable of behaving in this
manner for an indefinite season. After which the collapse is bril-
liant and total. Something of this sort had happened to me. Yet to
fathom what I had lost, what she had deprived me of, is hard to
say. I found its symptoms, but not the sickness which it was.

Medusa (I must call her that, she has no other name I know),
struck by the extraordinary arrow of her misfortune, condemned
to her relentless, uncanny, horrible isolation, her tragedy most
deeply rooted in the fact that she was not a myth, not a fabulous
and glamorous monster. . . . For it came to me one night in a
bar in Corinth, to consider if the first Medusa might have been
also such a victim, felled by some awesome fit, not petrifying but
petrified, so appalling to the eyes and, more significantly, to the
brooding aesthetic spirit that lives in man that she too was
shunned and hated and slain by a murderer who would observe
her only in a polished surface.

I spent some while in bars that summer. And later, much later,
when the cold climate of the year's end closed the prospect of
travel and adventure, I became afraid for myself, that dreadful
writer's fear which has to do with the death of the idea, with the
inertia of hand and heart and mind. Like one of the broken leaves,
the summer's withered plants, I had dried. My block was sheer. I
had expected a multitude of pages from the island, but instead I
saw those unborn pages die on the horizon, where the beach met
the sea.

And this, merely a record of marble, water, a plastic shell
strapped across a woman's face, this is the last thing, it seems,
which I shall commit to paper. Why? Perhaps only because she
was to me such a lesson in the futility of things, the waiting fist of
chance, the random despair we name the World.

And yet, now and then, I hear that voice of hers, I hear the way
she spoke to me. I know now what I heard in her voice, which had
neither pain nor shame in it, nor pleading, nor whining, nor even a
hint of the tragedy—the Greek tragedy—of her life. And what I
heard was not dignity either, or acceptance, or nobleness. It was

contempt. She despised me. She despised all of us who live without her odds, who struggle with our small struggles, incomparable to hers. "Your Greek is very good," she said to me with the patronage of one who is multilingual. And in that same disdain she says over and over to me: "That you live is very good." Compared to her life, her existence, her multilingual endurance, what are my life or my ambitions worth? Or anything.

It did not occur immediately, but still it occurred. In its way, the myth is perfectly accurate. I see it in myself, scent it, taste it, like the onset of inescapable disease. What they say about the gorgon is true. She has turned me to stone.

Introduction

Steve Rasnic Tem returns with another pure Shadows *story, concerning an old theme done to a turn.*

STONE HEAD

by Steve Rasnic Tem

He woke up with a severe headache. A migraine, he thought in surprise. He thought he had finally escaped their daily torment years ago. The room was soot-black, bone-black. He wasn't sure if it was because there was no moon or if the migraine had addled his senses. He could recall headaches so bad he could not speak, hear, or think.

Someone was speaking his name.

Had he overslept? Was it dark outside? For some reason he thought perhaps it might be early morning, just past midnight, but he could not find the window shade, did not even know where to look. It could be dawn outside his room; it could be noon. The headache seemed to be slowly creeping through the tissues of his brain, turning his brain—his thoughts—into stone.

Someone was speaking his name.

He knew his wife was not with him, knew without even touching that she was absent from her place beside him in the bed. He was not sure if she actually no longer lived with him; he had intended to divorce her many times, over a span of years. But something had always stopped him. Had he finally gone through with it? She had intended to divorce him as well, from time to time. She was fed up with his coldness, his distance, his lack of deep affection, she had said. Had she finally left him?

He did not know. He could not remember.

Someone was speaking his name.

He imagined he could hear the voice, but for some reason

thought perhaps he was merely thinking the words. But he could not picture the words. He could not remember his name.

Nor could he remember what he had been doing the previous day, the previous week, the month. He could not remember what he had been doing the past several years. He had not been happy, he thought. Perhaps that had been his condition. He felt that almost assuredly he had been alone.

Someone was speaking his name.

No, perhaps they were merely writing it. Yes, that was it! At last he could be sure of something! Someone was writing his name.

But why so loudly? Why was the process of writing his name so loud? Each stroke was a thundering inside his head. That was the source of his migraine—someone writing his name in this loud, pounding, thunderous way.

But yet, what had happened? He felt sure the previous day had been normal. He had gotten up, washed, dressed . . . Or perhaps he had not dressed, perhaps he had stayed in bed that day to read. Perhaps he had stayed in bed every day for several years, reading, sleeping . . .

No, he told himself, yesterday had been a normal day. It must have been a normal day. But now someone was writing his name. So loudly it was giving him a headache. And so severe a headache, he could not see. Everything was black.

What had happened to all his children? He could not remember. He knew he had not seen any of them in a long time, such a long time that he had, in fact, forgotten how many children there had been. Ungrateful lot, all of them—of that he was sure. But he could not remember their faces, could not remember their names. His memory had turned to stone.

Someone was pounding his name.

Of that, too, he was sure. His head quaked with each beat, each metronomic slam of his name, his signature. He could not feel his hands—was it he himself doing the pounding? He had signed checks, letters, so many checks for ungrateful children, an unfaithful wife. A wonder he had not written his signature permanently into his desk, etched it in. Perhaps it was his own hand, making his own signature, beating it, pounding each stroke of his signature into the ancient wood.

Someone was beating his name.

Bam! Bam! Bam! But it wasn't quite wood, was it? The surface he could hear was not wood, not ancient wood, not hard wood. Maybe metal . . . his wife pounding on the motel bathroom door he'd locked himself behind. Nagging, nagging, pound, pound, pound. His son . . . he had a son, working on that trashy car, pound, pound, pound. He thought his head would split. He could barely hear his own thoughts beneath the drumming.

Someone was cutting his name.

He could feel it on his arms, his thighs, his buttocks. The knife carving his initials. One of his daughters, painted to her wrists in his blood. Yes, yes, he knew the beat, beat, of her cutting, cut, cut, his initials, his initials. He tried to read his initials through his pain. But could not, could not . . .

Someone is chiseling his name.

. . . could not because it wasn't on his arms, his buttocks, at all. But beat, beat, beating into his forehead. His head again! Someone actually beating on his head, dulling his thinking, making it hard to live. He had no life! They didn't care!

Someone is chiseling his name. Someone is beating his name. Someone is chiseling his name.

His thoughts turn to stone. His memory turns to stone. There is no one. He has lost them all. He does not know how long ago they left. But there is no one. His thoughts are stone. His feelings are stone.

Someone is chiseling his name.

Someone is chiseling his name.

Into his forehead. Into his brain. At last he thinks he sees something: the name, his name, in front of him. On his forehead. His name is being written onto his forehead and yet he can see it, see up through his stone brain into his transparent forehead. Head stone. Where someone is chiseling his name. Someone is chiseling his name.

Someone is chiseling his name.

And the stonecutter is beautiful. The man has powerful arms. The stonecutter's chisel is silver, a sliver of moon.

Someone is chiseling his name.

As he sinks into the hole, as his arms grasp the sides of the hole and he begins to drift beneath the earth. As he looks into his forehead and sees his name being chiseled on the expanse of cool, white stone . . .

Someone is speaking his name.

Introduction

Alan Ryan, editor of the massive anthology Perpetual Light *and author of* Panther! *and* The Kill, *has worked as a teacher, theatrical publicist, and salesman at Macy's. Though he began as a writer of sf, he had moved almost exclusively into the realm of Dark Fantasy, one of the few writers who can wield a bludgeon and a razor at the same time.*

PIETÀ

by Alan Ryan

Fioretta's father raised skinny goats and spindly cows and clamorous chickens on the dusty hillsides of the Abruzzi overlooking Vasto and the Adriatic. From the front door of the house, Fioretta could look far out to the west and there, sparkling in the bright sunshine, was the deep and distant blue of the sea. Below, where the hills sloped down to the water's edge, were the gray- and white-plastered buildings of Vasto Marina and the hard white line of the beach. And all around were the hills, dotted, like her own, with farms. From the time she was a child old enough to think so and to say so, Fioretta had wanted nothing different for herself, but her father's brother, Zi' Carlo, was a priest and he would not have it so.

Una ragazza santa, he called her, a holy child, and often when he said it, especially when his brother's wine had flowed generously with the Sunday meal, his voice, heavy with piety, made it clear that he meant a child-saint.

When Fioretta was little, she would giggle and pull at Zi' Carlo's ear when he said this. Her laughter filled the house and seemed to mingle with the aromas of cooking and of animals to make the air brighter. She was happy. She was thrilled, like her father and mother and all others in her family, to have one of their own blood a priest. On Sundays, when Zi' Carlo came to dinner with his brother's family, her father always insisted that the two of them walk up and down in the roadway that led to the house. Her father knew what he was doing. The road wound in lazy loops up the side of the hill and anyone walking on it could be seen clearly from the valley below or from the hillsides opposite, the shimmering afternoon sun outlining their figures against the dusty yellow of the road. It was a good and proud thing to have a priest in the family, a priest of one's own blood.

On such occasions, Fioretta would walk with them, at Zi' Carlo's insistence, and her uncle would tell her colorful and wonderful tales of saints and martyrs. Fioretta would listen, wide-eyed, for Zi' Carlo was a marvelous storyteller. When finally her child's mind would grow tired, however, Zi' Carlo would send her on her way with a blessing—his knuckles, as he made the sign of the cross, were as knotted as those of his farmer-brother—and watch her run across the flower-dotted field to the house, bare elbows and heels flashing in the sun. Una ragazza santa, he would sigh.

Fioretta loved the farm. She loved the animals, even the mindless chickens, and the way the colors changed through the growing seasons and the way the air changed and the animals changed and gave birth to their young. She needed no urging to rise from her bed in the mornings. She would not miss the dawn; only sickness could keep her from it. She did her chores with a will. The farm, the farm, it was all she ever wanted.

But as she grew older, her father and uncle began to talk of sending her away.

At first, they spoke of sending her to a convent where she could be close to God who clearly had blessed her with such a rich soul. The talk persisted for several years while Fioretta grew, but it faded away when the child's ability with words and numbers and anything associated with school or learning or books proved more than she could master. She was a simple child. And she was relieved when the matter was dropped for a while.

Then talk began of something else. Zi' Carlo said that, simple though she was, Fioretta's heart was great, she was filled with love for God, clearly she was una ragazza santa, the holiest child he had ever seen in his years as a priest, and she must lead a life of service to God and to the Church. Certe, certe, her father said, his head nodding in time with his steps as he walked with his brother in the road. Across the field, among the dozing cows, Fioretta watched them in silence.

At last they told her. Fioretta lowered her eyes. She was an obedient child, an ornament, certainly, to any good family, her uncle told her father. But she could not enter the convent, she murmured slowly. The books were so hard. . . . Yes, that was true, the men agreed, but her uncle knew the good sisters who worked in Roma and helped to serve in the papal palace. Work for the pope? In Roma? In the house of the pope himself? Her uncle smiled. There is much to do, he reminded her, in the house of the Lord.

But the farm? Fioretta asked. Who will care for the cows and feed the chickens? Her voice could barely shape the words in the still air of the afternoon.

But every question had an answer and Fioretta, an obedient child, was, after a while, silent.

On the third day following her sixteenth birthday, accompanied by her mother's sister, Fioretta went to Roma to serve in the house of the Lord.

Roma bewildered and frightened her.

Around her in a dizzying circle swung the traffic, the buses, the people. People without faces or names filled the narrow streets and spilled over into the roads. Policemen frightened her, and the soldiers, endless Italian soldiers in bright and shiny uniforms, no two alike. And the chatter of foreign tongues, like the rattle of the devil's voice behind her. Twice she ventured out alone on her one day off in the week, explored the streets near her home without ever leaving sight of her landmark corner, and then went out no more.

From the single window in her tiny room on the fourth floor of the house she lived in, she could, if she strained a little past the window frame, see between two taller buildings the narrow brown ribbon of the Po. That, and the route from her house to the Vatican, was all she knew of Roma.

Six days of the week, she washed floors and polished furniture in the Vatican offices and apartments. At first, the lemon scent of the polish reminded her of the fruit trees at home, but soon she became accustomed to it and noticed it no more.

Three times in her first three months in Roma, Zi' Carlo came to visit her. On his first visit, she noticed with surprise how very much he resembled her father. The lines in his face were the same, his eyes the same shape, and the network of shadows around them. Only his mouth was really different, tighter, it seemed, and his laugh dryer, as if the old priest suffered from a fever.

"You work well?" he asked on his first visit.

"Oh, yes," Fioretta answered, her eyes averted.

"The work is agreeable to you, yes?"

"Si, Zi' Carlo," she said. "Yes."

They were standing in the shadow of San Pietro, near the little shop that sold Vatican postage stamps, with the motors of tour buses growling like beasts across the open piazza. Fioretta thought how the oil from the buses and their heavy black tires would stain the bright, hot concrete beneath them. Who washed the stones of the piazza? Fioretta wondered for an instant.

Zi' Carlo smiled down at her and placed one hand on the top of her head.

"You pray, yes?" he asked.

Fioretta nodded, and felt his hand move with her. Her hair, pulled back in a tight bun and flat on the top of her head, felt suddenly hot. "Yes."

"Good, good," Zi' Carlo said. "How happy you make me! And, child, remember always that your work is in itself a kind of prayer."

"Yes, uncle," she said. "I know it."

"As long as you are happy," said her uncle, the priest and brother of her father, and patted her twice on the head. He moved his hand and, smiling still, patted her twice on the cheek.

One true happiness she had, and one only.

She loved San Pietro and spent her free day—and, she whispered to her confessor, a few stolen hours as well—in its echoing cavern. With slow-moving feet, she traced in its cool marble floor the tiled outlines of the world's great churches, all of them smaller than hers. She patrolled the walls, drinking in the pictures and statues and textures of stone and light. She trembled for the saints and the martyrs and the pains they suffered. She visited the popes, ancient and recent, in the crypt and asked them to name her in their prayers. She craned her neck for long minutes to study the details of Bernini's marble and bronze baldachino above the high altar, where only the pope himself could say mass. She lost herself in dizzying visions of the dome. She loved the colored marbles and the gilt and fresco decorations. She loved San Pietro. And most of all she loved the Pietà.

Another girl who scrubbed floors in the Vatican offices, a girl from the north near San Marino, told her a terrible story. Not many years before, a crazy man had run up to the statue and hit it with a hammer, breaking pieces of marble from it. Look at the Virgin's hand, the girl told her, look at the Virgin's finger. Broken. It was broken right off, but the crazy man was caught and punished and the broken pieces were put back on. If you look very close, you can almost see the tiny lines where the pieces were put back in place. The Virgin's left hand, the one that sticks out like this, the girl said. She stuck her hand out, miming the posture of the statue, and giggled. Fioretta was stunned. She hadn't known, hadn't noticed.

How could a person do that, even a crazy person? Imagine attacking the milky white marble of the statue. She shivered at the thought and murmured a hasty prayer. She would have to look more closely at the Virgin's finger, she thought, as she glanced quickly down at her own left hand. The guards knew her. They would let her get close enough to see when there was no crowd around the statue. She had to see for herself this violation that she almost felt in her own limbs.

The next time she could, she went to the Pietà. The statue seemed almost to glow in the dim light.

Fioretta knelt on the hard cool floor before the Pietà, eyes searching and piercing the gloom of the corner, just to the right of the entrance, where the figure had stood for all these hundreds of years. The crowds were gone now. The guard, a nice man named

Eduardo who reminded her of her father—but, curiously, not at all of her uncle—glanced briefly at her, smiled, and strolled away. He had once told Fioretta that he had a daughter just the same age as her. Only when the sound of his steps had moved away did Fioretta look in his direction. Then her eyes came back to the white marble figure of the suffering mother.

White marble trembled like living flesh. Fioretta caught her breath. No, she had only imagined it. But the figures were so real, so very real. Her eyes started over again, traveling across the features of mother and son, catching at details like fingers at a thread. The angle of the mother's head was itself enough to bring a tear. The exhaustion of her body. The delicate thinness of her hands. So young. Fioretta swallowed a lump in her throat and blinked back the blur from her eye.

White marble trembled like living flesh.

And the son. Lifeless. The body sagging under its own emaciated weight. Ribs countable. Arm limp. Head lolling to the side. Fioretta wondered what it weighed. It. Wondered what it weighed. Heavy for the sorrowing mother, but otherwise light as dust.

White marble trembled like living flesh.

Fioretta rose slowly from her knees—knees stiff with long kneeling on stone floors—and took one tentative step closer. She paused, her breath coming quickly, and glanced over her shoulder. She saw one figure in the distance, Eduardo, she thought, but no one else. She turned back to the statue, took another step, and another. She moved to the right, toward the head of the son and the mother's outstretched hand, outstretched broken finger.

White marble trembled like living flesh.

She thought, only just thought, she could see the crack that marked the break in the finger. More suffering, even in stone. Fioretta stood still, balanced on the balls of her feet, plucked at a few more details unseen before, then straightened, sighed, shivered for an instant.

"Madre di Dio . . ." she murmured, and realized she had no breath for whispered prayer. She stood in silence another moment, then backed off three steps before turning to leave the church.

Behind her, she knew, white marble trembled like living flesh.

"Ti piace?" Zi' Carlo asked, and gestured toward the statue.

"Sì, Zio," she answered softly. "It is my favorite."

"Your favorite!" he exclaimed happily. "Ah! Ah! I knew my niece would have good taste. Of course, of course. Yes, this is the most beautiful statue in the world, a work of the truly inspired imagination. It is to your credit that you recognize it, niece." He looked briefly at the gleaming figure of mother and son. "Che belezza!" he said emphatically. Then he looked at the girl. "E che santa ragazza."

Fioretta's eyes lingered, caressing the statue, as they moved away to pray before the dried remains of long-dead fathers of the Church.

Fioretta missed the farm and she was lonely.

Far, far away, the cows and goats still grazed the hill, the chickens pecked in the dusty yard, and tiny purple flowers colored the fields. Below the hills, the city of Vasto slumbered, beneath the cliff Vasto Marina dozed by the water and sand, and the blue Adriatic, just visible from the door of her house on the hill, still twinkled in the sun, like daytime stars swallowed by the waves.

On her free afternoon, Fioretta sat by the window, elbows on the stone ledge, and craned her neck outside. In the growing gloom of evening, she could just make out the mud of the Po, snaking past the buildings that crowded her view.

It became her habit to visit the statue at night. By now, all the guards knew her at least by sight, if not by name. A strange one, said a few. But others recognized the girl as being like many they had seen come and go before her. These kept silent and looked the other way while Fioretta kept her vigil in the near total darkness.

She thought sometimes of the farm. She thought how, if she could be there, she would hold the farm the way the mother held the son.

In the dim light of the corner, the white milky marble glowed and shimmered before her tearful eyes.

She unclasped her hands and knelt up straight. If she reached out now, she could touch . . . it. She could touch it. Touch the body of the son. She raised one hand, one finger outstretched, and . . . touched it.

What she touched was soft and warm.

Her hand, her finger, stiff with sudden fright, remained where they were.

The marble yielded beneath the soft pressure of her fingertip. She was touching the twisted, narrow chest. Beneath the . . . flesh . . . Beneath the flesh, she felt the bone of a rib. It did not move with the warm breath of life, but the flesh continued to yield to her finger.

Eyes wide, unblinking, she turned her gaze slowly to the face. A tiny trickle of blood ran from the son's nose, drew a dark line from nose to mouth, and ran between the slightly parted lips.

Fioretta recoiled from the body. And recoiled again, realizing that she had thought of it as a body. She blinked once and looked, breath still tight in her chest. It was a body. Her eyes swept up the details. Flesh the color of flesh even in the dim light. Soiled, once-white cloth draped across the loins. Wrenched muscles and tendons. The lifeless sag of the stomach, the breathless rigidity of the chest, the unfeeling droop of the head. She could see the length and curl of the dark eyelashes, blood and mud in the matted hair. A broken blister gleamed wetly on the back of one hand. The lower lip was swollen and raw. The right eye was blackened and the right ear filled with dark, dried blood. She had never seen these things before.

She let out one long slow breath and carefully withdrew her hand. It hesitated, hovered near the body, moved slowly toward the bony shoulder, and touched it. Still warm. Still yielding, with bone still hard beneath it.

Her lips moved but there was no prayer with words for this.

Heart pounding, she stared at the body. Then she thought of the mother. She looked up quickly. The Virgin was still stone, milky white in the dim light.

Silence cloaked Fioretta. No step moved near her. No voice.

She closed her eyes. Opened them. The mother was still marble, the son still dead.

A thought—one clear, specific thought—rose in Fioretta's mind. The body, she thought, cannot be left here. Crazy people will come and attack it. I have to take it away. And with the thought still shimmering like dark crystal in her mind, she stepped forward, arms out, and grasped with her right hand the legs and with her left hand the shoulders.

Moving without further thought, she slipped her arms beneath the yielding dead weight of the body—feeling the hard coolness of the marble mother on the backs of her hands—and lifted it against her stomach. It was lighter than she expected—about the same weight as a calf, she thought for an instant—but still she staggered back a step before she found her balance beneath the burden.

Out, she had to take it out of here.

It was only a few steps to the front entrance, the great main doors, and she was almost to them before she halted in sudden panic. Her awkward movement made the body shift in her straining grasp and one of the dead arms swung loose and rapped her on the leg.

She looked back at the dark interior of the basilica. No one. But she could not just walk out the front door of San Pietro with the body of the Christ in her arms, the body that was supposed to be a statue. The statue. She looked toward the corner. The sorrowful mother bent her head over empty arms. And Fioretta was suddenly calm. What was the mother intending to do? She meant to bury her son. The girl looked down, for the first time, at the bruised and bloody face of the dead man in her arms. Peace. There was peace in the face. She looked up again at the huge doorway and began walking steadily toward it. Once she hitched the body higher in her arms, and once she thought that the blood would stain her clothing, but her step did not falter.

She reached the doorway. It was late now, the day dimmed into evening, and the great open piazza was empty. She stood in the doorway, breathing heavily with the strain of carrying the corpse, then walked the few paces forward to the edge of the first step. The weight dragged at her arms and shoulders and as she walked, her foot kicked something solid but yielding. The hand, she thought, the swinging, lifeless hand. She hesitated in mid-step, then shifted the corpse higher as best she could. Carefully she continued down the stone steps, leaving behind the shelter of the great doorway and the darkness of the shadows.

Only when she was outside, her feet touching the stones of the piazza, did she realize that the doors of San Pietro should not have been open at this hour. But she did not look back. She aimed her wavering gaze at the great obelisk of Heliopolis in the center of the piazza and walked slowly toward it.

Her arms were growing numb. A tingling filled her left hand and her wrist was caught at a painful angle. But she could not set the burden down, she thought, lest she be unable to hoist it up again. With every fifth or sixth step, she tried to lift the body higher, but each such movement brought new pain to her wrist and now her fingers were growing cramped. A sharp pain stabbed through her left shoulder and a dull one filled her right. As she walked, the pain slipped down from her shoulders and caught at her back. Her knees grew shaky and uncertain, her feet heavy. She bit her lower lip with the effort, but soon found that she couldn't breathe enough unless her mouth were open. She opened her mouth wide and tried to suck in enough air to sustain her. She was halfway across the piazza. She had given no thought to where she was going, but she saw now that she was heading toward her house, toward her room, the only place she knew in all of Roma. Breathe. Step. Hitch the weight higher. Breathe. Step.

Someone walked toward her out of the night.

Fioretta stopped, stood still, heard her own ragged breath, sucked in air, blinked as stinging sweat ran from her hair into her eye. A man. A policeman. What would he say when he saw her?

The figure came closer, step, step, closer, came walking toward her and passed right by her elbow.

She half turned to stare in amazement but the weight in her arms made it difficult to move. Walked right past her. Am I not here? she wondered. Do I not stand here with the body of Christ in my arms?

The weight of the body compelled her forward again. Step. Breathe. Step.

And halt again as another figure floated toward her from another direction, crossing the piazza on a path that would intersect hers. She stood, panting, and waited. The figure, a soldier this time, came closer, looked at her, looked through her, never saw her, never halted, walked on out of sight behind her.

"Madre di Dio, sono morta," she said, and caught at the air she had used to say it.

The weight of the body dragged mercilessly at her arms. A wrenching pain cut at the small of her back. A stitch nipped at her side. Her breath came in gulps of hot air.

Other people, distant shadows, moved across the piazza. Some looked toward her briefly but none seemed to see her.

Fioretta lowered her head closer to her burden. The scent of urine caught at her nose and throat. She kept walking, steady pace, breathe, step, breathe, step.

And came to the door of her house.

Home, she thought, not the home I would choose, but home. Oh, she thought, if this were the hillside and the farm, I would bury you with singing and prayers beneath purple flowers in sight of the sea.

The door on the street was open. Never was this door left open, for fear of thieves and evil, but this night it was open.

Fioretta stumbled inside toward the dark stairs, started up, and her foot kicked the dead hand once again. She stopped, leaned, panting, on the grimy wall, the new pressure on her shoulder bringing no relief, only new pain to her bursting, burning shoulder. Oh, Madre di Dio, she thought, help me up the stairs. With one final lurch, she stood away from the wall, thought for a terrifying instant that she would lose her balance and topple over with the corpse, then caught herself, steadied herself, tried to calm her breathing, gathered her muscles and her remaining strength and lifted the corpse higher for one last time.

When she reached the fourth floor—she could not spare the effort to count but her leaden feet knew the way home—the door of her room was open. It swung back slowly at the pressure of her shoulder and she turned sideways to slip in with her burden, taking care that the dead man's head would pass through without knocking. But the feet caught on the door and the weight almost slipped from her arms. Her own arms almost numb, she caught quickly at it, found another smokelike wisp of strength, and stood in the middle of her tiny room, the corner of the bed touching her leg. With a groan, she leaned forward and let the body slide from her arms onto the bed. But even with the burden gone, it was some minutes before her screaming back permitted her to straighten up. When she did, she had to brace herself against the wall to keep from collapsing.

She looked at the shadowy figure that filled the grayness of her bed. It will stain the bed with blood, she thought. But she was too exhausted to think about it further. Her eyes closed. After a moment, she forced them open and at the same time forced a long breath deep into her burning lungs.

The body lay dark on the bed.

Fioretta wanted to do more, wanted to arrange the limbs decently, make certain the eyes were closed, fold the hands across the stomach, wipe the blood from the face. No strength. She had no strength. Trailing one hand on the gritty plaster of the wall, she slipped slowly to the floor and, knees drawn up to her chest, closed her eyes and slept at last.

In the morning, the body was gone. Where it had lain, the bed was smooth.

Fioretta knelt on the floor beside the bed and stared, stared at the untouched covers, stared where the stains should have been, searched and searched but found nothing. In disbelief, she ran her hand lightly across the bed, half expecting still to find the body grown somehow invisible. Nothing.

"Oh, Madre di Dio," she whispered, but found no further words.

Her arms and back and shoulders still ached with the strain of the night before.

When she reached San Pietro, the statue of mother and son gleamed cool white. Fioretta did not go near it, only stared unmoving from the doorway.

All morning she polished furniture and in the afternoon washed floors. The oily smell of the furniture polish almost sickened her. The rough edges of the mosaic floor, made uneven by decades and decades of walking, scratched and tore at her knuckles. Three times she had to wipe her own blood from the tiles. She was hardly aware of the pain. The three outer fingers of her left hand were still numb. Her right hand, buffing the colored tiles and chips

of stone, moved of its own volition, news that it was moving coming to Fioretta's mind only through the searing, swelling waves of
pain in her shoulder.

That night she went back to San Pietro.

And the statue gleamed cool white.

Mother and son.

Pietà.

Fioretta looked around. None of the guards were in sight. She
stood alone with mother and son. Around her, San Pietro was as
silent as the hills of the Abruzzi.

She stepped closer and, wondering, touched it, and, shivering,
felt its warmth.

She wailed this time in dread, a high, keening note but soft and
low in her throat. There was no one to hear but the marble
mother and the dead ears of the murdered son.

She touched it again. Still warm.

Why will you not be buried? she thought. If only this were the
farm, you could lie so still and quiet beneath the purple flowers.

And finally she leaned forward, sighing heavily, and slipped her
right arm beneath the knees and her left beneath the shoulders
and felt the weight tugging her over, but stood and carried her
burden, she and it invisible, across the piazza and through the
streets of the darkened city, past the ghostly, sightless people in
the piazza, back to her house, her room, her bed.

This time she touched the face, felt the crusted blood and the
swollen tissue.

And this time she wept before sleeping.

And in the morning, the body was gone.

She worked all day, head throbbing, muscles knotted, knees
threatening to abandon her, stomach on the edge of heaving,
sweat chilling her forehead.

And in the night, when she returned to San Pietro to see—she
had to see—the marble mother wept silently again over her dead
son.

And Fioretta wept with her.

And touched the still-warm body.

And lifted it again in her arms.

And, staggering, carried it, laid it to rest on her bed, and slept once again on the floor, wishing for the hills and the farm.

And in the morning, the body was gone.

And in the night, San Pietro called her. The marble itself, the cold, dead marble called her.

And in the morning . . .

And in the night . . .

And in the morning . . .

And in the night . . .

Introduction

Al Sarrantonio, whose stories have appeared in Analog, Heavy Metal, Terrors, *and* Shadows 4, *among other publications, returns to the series with a story as unnerving as it seems to be straightforward. But there is seldom anything straightforward about the adventures of young boys; it is only in nostalgic retrospect that youth appears to have been simple—and nonthreatening.*

BOXES

by Al Sarrantonio

They went to see the man who collected boxes.

There were two of them, Nathan and Roger, and they went in the afternoon after lunch and armed with flashlights and code kits. They carried Boy Scout Handbooks in their ski coat pockets, and candybars and a railroad flare which Roger had stolen from his father's workbench. Nathan had a whistle ring and two sticks of gum which he hoarded to himself. They went in October, when the sun was orange-red and large as a hanging jack-o'-lantern, and they went in the afternoon when the leaves danced circles at their feet in the curt wind and when the chill of winter death was beginning to settle in on porches and doorsteps. They went with caps on their heads, and the energetic joy of the young bloomed in their cheeks and in their bright angel eyes.

Sidewalks disappeared under their running feet. Nathan leaped at the near-nude branch of a tree, missing it with an ooof. Roger leaped behind him and touched it.

The wind whistled the dark day's passing.

The man who collected boxes lived at the far end of the farthest block. His house—lonely, square, and brooding—suddenly reared up before them, and they skidded to a halt.

Roger looked at Nathan.

This was the dividing line, the place where innocent adventure stopped and the breaking of rules began. Bicycles were not even allowed to be ridden to this spot. Cats shied away. The lawn around the house of the man who collected boxes was immaculately trimmed, green even in this late time of the year. No dog did his business here.

No tree grew here.

Nathan and Roger shied away from the perfect, straight front walk, crept instead across the forbidden lawn. Breathing lightly, they drew up to the side of the house. Gingerbread brown it was, and seemed still wet to the touch it looked so freshly painted. So fresh that Roger found himself reaching to touch it. Nathan slapped at his hand and motioned for him to be quiet. Roger smiled.

Around to the back they crept, stopping underneath the one window. Shivers went through them both.

They raised their heads.

Inside, dimly lit, were the colors of Christmas morning. Red and green, gold and bronze, silver, blue.

Boxes.

There they were. Stacked one upon the other, butted up against walls, on tables and chairs, filling almost every inch of space. Boxes. Enameled and lacquered, painted in watercolor, pastel, and crayon, of wood, of cardboard, of tin and beaten brass, round, square, oval, triangle, large, little, tiny, nested, oblong, flat, high, decorated with stencils or drawings, some plain, some elaborately carved, lidded, unlidded, hinged, fitted, some with brass pulls, some with brass handles, some with moldings of party colors, others green felt-lined, red felt-lined, violet felt-lined, black felt-lined, flat-topped and dome-topped, pyramid-topped, untopped, some with secret compartments, keys, spring locks, one with a tiny steel padlock, with stained-glass insets, clear-glass insets, round peek holes, false tops, one with stubby teak legs, one with the face of a monkey tattooed to its front, one with the head of a camel carved from its lid-pull, one with trick eyes set into its side that seemed to follow you back and forth, one with a knife spring-jacked into its bottom, ready to fly up on opening, one with tactile poison along its ridged lip, one with the face of a happy clown on its cover that changed to a frown when you turned it upside down. A bright pink one with peeling paint. A chocolate-colored one with a crack in one corner. One that had never been opened—and never could be. One that had never been closed. One encrusted with precious gems: rubies, a topaz, sapphires, a thumb-sized diamond, eight-sided.

Nathan and Roger stared, fascinated, into the room and their eyes made a glue bond with these boxes. This was part of the dream of their plan. To see these boxes. To peer into this forbidden window and witness the treasures of the man who collected boxes.

To be among them.

There was no communication between Nathan and Roger. Their souls were united and separate in this decision. They had come to observe and now they must touch. Boy Scout Handbooks were fumbled out of slick ski parka pockets and paged through. How to open a stuck window? As expected, there was nothing on how to open a closed window, especially one that did not belong to the scout doing the opening. Handbooks went back into pockets, and Roger, in a sudden and triumphant flash of thought, produced a small scout knife, attached to his keychain. It pulled open into a one-inch blade. Nathan was doubtful, but Roger overrode his doubt with enthusiasm.

Eyes peered over the window ledge again.

Boxes beckoned.

With care and the special skill of an amateur, Roger slipped the knife blade under the rubber seal of the outside window and tried to pry it out. Nathan suddenly grabbed his arm, stopping him. He pointed. There was a catch on the horizontal window, and it was in the open position.

Roger pocketed his tiny knife and pulled the window to the side.

It opened with a smooth hiss.

Nathan and Roger exchanged glances.

Behind them, the wind whipped up. An early moon had risen,

and shone a pale crescent at their backs. The red sun was sinking. The sky had deepened a notch on the blue color scale, toward eventual black. The air bit cold.

Nathan looked at Roger and thought suddenly of home. Of Dad at six o'clock, coming home with a quart of milk, of the paperboy, of television, of the warm couch and the sharp smell of supper and Mom moving about in the next room. Of sister upstairs, playing her records too loud. Of an apple or late-peach pie, cooling by the kitchen window; the window open a crack to cool the pie but keep the chill out. Of his schoolbooks waiting in his room, neatly stacked; the neon lamp waiting to be buzzed on. Dad reading his paper and the smell of coffee. A warm bed with a crazyquilt coverlet Mom made last winter. The ticking sound of heat coming up in the baseboard. Thoughts of Halloween coming and Thanksgiving coming and Christmas coming. Kickball at recess tomorrow. Late-peach pie and cold milk.

Nathan turned to go and Roger took his arm. A look of reproach crossed his face. Somewhere at the other end of the block a dog barked once, twice. Roger held on to Nathan's arm, pulled his gaze back to the window.

To the boxes inside.

The dog barked again but Nathan did not hear it. Roger looked at him and smiled. Nathan made a step with his hands, locking them together and cradling Roger's foot, hoisting him up and over the ledge. There was momentary silence, and then Roger's face appeared on the other side. He was still smiling. He reached down for Nathan, who now locked his hands in Roger's hands and pulled himself up, over, and in.

Nathan righted himself and heard Roger sliding the window shut behind them.

There was almost nowhere to turn or step. There were boxes to the ceiling. Nathan tried to move deeper into the room and nearly knocked over a large box with carved pull knobs and black polka dots painted on its yellow surface. It tilted and began to fall toward a pile of black lacquer boxes which were stacked upon a cardboard storage box with rope handles. Nathan grabbed at it with both hands, noting its smooth and dustless finish, and righted it.

Roger, meanwhile, had found a pathway of sorts through the boxes and was disappearing behind a bronze-cornered trunk. Nathan hurried to catch up to him.

They both found themselves in a hurricane eye in the center of the room, a tiny cleared out spot walled in on all sides by boxes. It was very dim here, since the fading outside light was cut off by a row of bloodred cubes of diminishing size, starting at the bottom at about three feet square and finishing at the top with a pyramid topper of a tiny box a half inch on a side. There was enough light to see, though, and Roger cut off Nathan's attempt to snap on his flashlight, indicating that it would ruin the effect by having their own light infringe on this treasure room.

Nathan demurred, then agreed.

They sat, Indian style, in their spot and reveled in the boxes. Roger leaned over to his right, plucking at an oval tin circled with painted swans. He opened it, gazed into its bright reflective insides, and closed it again. Nathan stared up at the skyline of boxes around them, and thought how wonderful a dream this would make. There were more colors and pleasing shapes here than anywhere on earth—there must be—and he could think of no place that was more dreamlike. Roger brushed his fingers over the mottled surface of an ebony shoebox-sized box and sighed.

Light became a little dimmer.

There was a sound, and Nathan and Roger were startled. They had forgotten that they had broken into the house of the man who collected boxes; they had forgotten altogether that there was a man connected with these boxes. That had been part of the original adventure—to see the boxes, but above all to see the man who collected them. This they would be able to tell their friends—that they had not only seen the boxes but, most of all, that they had seen the man in the perfect house who kept them.

The sound came again.

It was almost a scrabbling sound—like tiny fiddler crabs loose in a wooden boat and ticking all over its inside surface. An ancient and wheezing sound—old age with claws, moving with slow careful grace and constant, inevitable movement toward its destination.

Nathan and Roger were trapped.

The sound was all around them—slow, inexorable—and, though

they were on their feet and fingering their Scout Handbooks, there was nowhere to turn. Nathan could not locate the pathway back to the window; indeed, that pathway had seemed to disappear and even the line of bloodred pyramid boxes no longer stood in quite the same line. The tin box Roger had handled was nowhere to be seen.

There was the sound of a box opening.

Somewhere behind them, or in front of them, or to their left or right. A large box with a large and ponderous lid was being opened. There was a heavy, wheezy breathing. A rattling, dry cough. Another wheezing breath, and then a whispered grunt and the closing of the box lid.

A shuffling sound, the click of a light switch, a shuffling sound once more.

The room was suffused with a dull amber glow, like that in a dusty antique shop. The colors of the boxes deepened and softened.

A dry cough and the shuffling continued.

Abruptly, from behind a box with the grey-painted form of an elephant on it, the man who collected boxes appeared.

Nathan and Roger drew back.

The man who collected boxes shuffled toward them and lifted his heavy head. There were wrinkles there, so many that his eyes were almost lost to view behind them. His hair was the color of white dandelion and looked as though it would, like dandelion, fly away if breathed upon. His hands were veined and trembling, his bones gaunt.

He lifted his head, slowly, and looked out at them through the black shadows of his eyes.

He tried to speak.

He lifted his hand, painfully, and opened his mouth, but only a rasp emerged, dry as yellowed newspaper.

His hand lowered itself to his side.

Nathan looked at Roger.

At that moment, the dog at the end of the block barked again, and Nathan heard it, muffled as it was. He looked at Roger. It was six o'clock.

Late-peach pie would be cooling.

Nathan felt Roger's hand on his arm, but he pulled away. In the pale yellow light he found the slight opening between a dull blue nest of boxes and a charcoal-colored case; he slipped sideways between them and made his way through the maze of boxes to the window, sliding it open. It showed a dark rectangle of the outside world.

He climbed quickly out, hesitating on the ledge.

The dog barked once more, sharply.

He jumped down onto perfect grass.

Behind him as he ran, he heard the shuffle of shoes, and then the clean sound of one lid closing, and then another.

Introduction

Avon Swofford lives in California, writes when she can and when she's nagged, and in this—her first professional sale—considers the possibility that shadows, both of the mind and of the wall, aren't always willing to go away when you ask them.

AND I'LL BE WITH YOU
BY AND BY

by Avon Swofford

Greg wasn't sure he knew exactly what he had invented. The machine was an accident, an attempt to use biofeedback and alpha waves. He liked to tinker with outlandish projects to counter the monotony of repairing household appliances. It wasn't a business exactly; he was more of an odd-jobman the local people called in to fix whatever wasn't still under warranty. He didn't make a lot of money, but he had plenty of free time and a fully stocked workshop that was deductible.

By late afternoon he had decided he'd put in enough work on electric toasters and had started working on his newest project. It wasn't much to look at: just a jumbled assortment of circuit boards, transistors, and wires. He had the headset on and was concentrating on the oscilloscope when suddenly he felt the presence of others. He worked to tune in the strange communications and then heard Oliver.

He knew immediately it was Oliver, not from the tone of voice —there was no voice—but somehow from the feel of the thoughts. After ten years, he still remembered; and in particular, he remembered Oliver's death.

His hands trembled as he removed the headset and took several deep breaths. He felt weak as he stood up from the worktable. Oliver's presence brought back painful memories. He had been riding in the car with Oliver when the accident occurred. Greg had come through without a scratch, but Oliver never regained consciousness, never spoke to Greg again—until now.

He went to the window and looked outside. Maybe someone had called to him, someone who sounded like Oliver. But the field was deserted and he could see no one through the barren trees lining the distant highway. He turned back to the machine. Something had triggered those memories. Somehow Oliver had come back to him.

He returned to the table and picked up the headset, not wanting to put it on again, yet unable to ignore the force of Oliver's presence. He had to know. Slowly he slipped it on.

At first he felt nothing; then Oliver was there. This time the thoughts were distinct.

"Oliver?" Greg asked.

"I'm here," Oliver answered. Greg felt no emotion, just a quiet sense of waiting. Oliver was giving him time, but there was also a sense of urgency to his thoughts.

He forced himself to relax and, as he concentrated, Oliver's presence became more concrete. He could almost see his friend: not a dim memory from ten years ago, but a clear image of Oliver at eighteen with long blond hair and dark eyes. He hadn't changed.

"How can I be talking to you? You died." Even as he said it, he could feel the fear. Oliver evidently felt it too and responded with alarm.

"Don't go—I have to talk to you."

"But you're dead." Greg spoke as if somehow Oliver had to be convinced. "You can't be here."

"I am," Oliver answered. "I'm here. Somehow you've managed to reach us."

Greg could feel a strange eagerness in Oliver's voice. "Us?" he asked.

"Us—those of us who are here."

What? Greg's question was unvoiced but Oliver understood.

"Dead, I suppose. Changed," he answered impatiently. "I can see you. I can see my parents and my brother. Can you imagine what it's like, waiting, begging for a chance to communicate?

You've got to get in touch with my parents. Bring them here."

"Who else is there?" Greg asked, his mouth dry at the thought that now ran through his head.

"I don't know—everyone, I suppose. Why are you so slow? I don't want to talk to you. Go. Get the others now."

The harshness in Oliver's voice frightened Greg so much he reached up and yanked the headset off. The commands had been almost mesmerizing, and the eerie way Oliver stared—his dark eyes never blinking, never wavering from Greg's face—unnerved him. He felt chilled even though the shed was well heated. Shivering, he hugged himself tightly and then glanced around the room to reassure himself nothing had changed. He had been so involved in the conversation that he'd lost all sense of time and place. Now it seemed odd to find himself back in familiar surroundings—odd, yet comforting.

He leaned back and gazed at the cluttered table almost in awe. Whatever it was he had built here was special, something uniquely his. He wished suddenly that his father could see it. Surely this would have impressed him. "Probably not," he said aloud and reached over to turn off the machine. He hesitated. Better leave it on, he thought. He wanted another opinion. Someone else should try it. It wouldn't do to break the connection. *Oliver wouldn't like it.* It was a quick thought, almost a subconscious one, but it frightened him and he pulled his hand abruptly from the switch, stood up and left the shed, closing the door behind him.

He walked across the driveway to the house, which was almost as rickety as the shed. It was a two-story building with peeling yellow paint and a wide veranda on both sides. It needed work but it had promise. That's what Beth had said. All old houses in Savannah had promise. Besides, she had added, there was a chance that this one had survived Sherman's army; surely it deserved their help.

History was Beth's hobby, just as electronics was Greg's. He didn't care much about Sherman's army. But the price was right, it was far enough from downtown Savannah, and the shed had been thrown in free. Greg had used the remainder of the inheritance money left by his father to buy it. So far, it had definitely been worth the investment.

He picked his way carefully through the jumble of old furniture and half-empty paint cans on the back porch. The encounter in the shed had taken longer than he realized and Beth was already home. He could hear her humming in the kitchen. She had taken off her winter coat, but her head was still hidden by a wool cap and scarf. The sight of her comforted him and he leaned against the doorjamb watching her unpack the groceries.

She was the practical one, always ready to deal with any situation. She'd come down from New Jersey to go to school and they'd met in an English class. He liked her immediately. Not her looks; she was a bit overweight and her hair hung straight and shapeless, but her briskness and efficiency impressed him. By the end of the semester, they were living together.

"What'd you bring me?" he asked.

"Middle of the month trip," she said, not looking up from the paper bags. "Nothing special, no meat, no ice cream. Sorry." When he didn't respond, she looked up and saw him staring. "Are you all right, Greg? You look tired."

"Been working out in the shed. I've stumbled onto something a little weird. I thought maybe you could help."

"A problem—with your electronics? I don't know anything about that stuff," she said.

"It's not electronics, it's more like psychology."

"That's supposed to be my specialty." She sat down and took off her scarf and cap. "What's up?"

He didn't speak immediately. She sensed his confusion and waited.

"Well, I've been working with the brain waves, biofeedback, that sort of stuff," he said finally. Beth nodded. "But what I got is different from anything I've ever felt. It's—" He paused, uncertain how to proceed. "I seem to be in communication with an old friend of mine. But there's just one problem. He's dead. He died almost ten years ago."

"What?" She drew away from him slightly, her eyes narrowing as she watched him. "Greg, that's—"

"No, listen," he interrupted. "It's true. At least it appears to be.

I was working with the frequencies and suddenly I felt him. At least I thought I did," he finished lamely. Beth studied his face for a moment.

"Were you thinking of him before you turned on the machine?" she asked. Gratefully, Greg relaxed. At least she wasn't laughing.

"No, I haven't thought about him in years. But as soon as I hit that frequency, I knew it was him. The feeling of him was so strong. I honestly don't think I could have imagined it."

"The mind is tricky. You can remember a lot of things."

"That's why I want you to try it. You didn't know him, so you shouldn't be able to feel him like I did."

She was silent for a moment, then stood up. "All right," she said. "Let's give it a try."

"Right now?" Greg realized he didn't want to go back to the shed now that it was getting dark. That shouldn't have made any difference, but it did.

Beth saw his hesitation. "It really spooked you, didn't it?"

"Spooked is the right word." He tried to laugh off her concern and his own. "It's not that important. Let's have dinner first."

"No, let's do it now," she said. "I want to know what's bothering you."

"All right," he agreed reluctantly and picked up his coat. He didn't want to go back outside. The shed seemed cold and forbidding. But she was right. He had to know what was out there. Whatever it was, she could handle it. He was sure of that. The thought made him even angrier at himself for holding back and he stepped out ahead of her, leading the way across the driveway.

When Greg reached the shed, he turned on all the lights, even the outside floodlight. Still, it seemed dark.

"Do you feel anything?" he asked.

"A little chilly," she answered, laughing. He smiled awkwardly in return and went to get the headset. Beth took it and settled easily in the tattered blue armchair next to the worktable.

"Relax," he said. It was unnecessary. She was relaxed. He was the one who was tense. She slipped on the headset and Greg leaned against the worktable to watch her. As she concentrated on the images, her face was blank and her eyes stared into the distance as if she were in a trance. Disturbed, Greg reached over and turned off the machine. He couldn't wait any longer; he had to have her reaction.

She wasn't angry or surprised that he had cut the connection. Rather, she appeared thoughtful as she removed the headset.

"Well?" he said impatiently while she sat silently, playing with the earphones.

"You say you know him?" she asked.

"You did talk to him then? There is something there?"

"Oh, there's something there all right. Someone, perhaps. The interesting thing is that you seem to know him. To me he's a stranger. The machine must affect the subconscious in different ways."

"It's not the subconscious. It can't be. You talked to him. It must be outside the mind of the person who uses it."

"It would appear that way, I'll admit," Beth said. "But I'm not willing to believe it yet. Communication with the dead, mediums, esp and all that garbage—this isn't the way it's supposed to work." She looked up at him. "Did he tell you anything about himself?"

"No," Greg said. "I guess I didn't really ask. I was so stunned to feel him in my mind like that. And to recognize him."

"Well, I asked some pretty specific questions, but he wouldn't answer. He's very anxious to get through to us, though. He wants his parents."

"Yeah, he mentioned that."

Beth leaned back in the armchair, still holding the headset. She seemed somewhat distracted.

"Do you want to talk to him again?" he asked.

"No," she answered quickly, and he realized that she did indeed share his sense of uneasiness. "I don't understand what we have here. I can't believe it and yet I can't deny it. We appear to be involved with some sort of telepathic communication."

"But with what?"

"That's what's frightening, isn't it," Beth said as she carefully laid the headset on the table. "You could accept it if it were with someone alive, but a ghost?" She stood up and moved away from the table, staring at the machine with obvious distaste. "And that's not all, Greg," she said. "Oliver knew who I was but I don't know him. I don't like the fact that he has the advantage."

"He's dying to get in touch with us," Greg said.

"Ha ha. Very funny. By the way, does the name 'Diangelo' mean anything to you?"

"It's Oliver's name. His last name."

"Did you ever mention that to me?"

"Hell no. I haven't thought about him in years."

"Well, there's some kind of transference going on, either between you and me or between me and Oliver."

Greg picked up the headset and laid it on top of the machine. He felt vulnerable in front of it, as though it were silently watching. "Let's go back to the house," he said. Beth nodded and turned toward the door. Greg stared at the machine for a moment longer before reaching behind it and pulling the plug. As he went out, he padlocked the door. Beth waited outside and they walked back to the house silently, her arm in his.

As they got ready for bed, Beth seemed quiet and pensive. The distant attitude Greg had sensed in her earlier had not diminished, yet she didn't mention Oliver again.

Finally, as they lay together in the darkness, he reached for her, but she pulled away. He sighed and lay down again.

"Tomorrow we'll know for sure," she said.

"What do you mean 'tomorrow'?" he asked.

"I asked Oliver to contact my brother. See if he's around up there."

"You what?" He sat up and stared at her. "You can't do that."

"Don't get upset, Greg." Puzzled, she looked at him. "Ben died when I was very young, about ten or so. I never knew him. Think about what a chance it is—I can finally meet my younger brother." She sounded as impatient as Oliver had. Greg began to shake his head in the dark. They were getting into this too fast.

"It can't hurt," she said. "Look, Greg, maybe it's just some sort of transference from your mind to mine. If so, then we'll know by tomorrow. But if it's not, then you will have bridged the widest gap there is. Everything will change."

"That's what I'm afraid of," he said softly. There were some gaps better left open, he thought. Beth didn't notice his hesitation. She sat up and kissed his shoulder.

"Tomorrow I'll talk to my brother and you'll call the Diangelos for Oliver. Then maybe he'll be in a better mood to answer our questions."

He said nothing and she lay back down and closed her eyes. He could only remember Mrs. Diangelo and the agony in her eyes as she had sat quietly at the funeral. Mr. Diangelo had cried. How could he tell them their dead son wanted to talk to them? What if he was wrong?

Beth was gone when Greg woke up. It was early, just barely daylight. He got up quickly and put on some clothes.

The machine was already on and she was sitting in the armchair. Her eyes were vacant, but tears streamed down her cheeks. Alarmed, he took off the headset and smoothed her hair. She seemed reluctant to return to reality and he waited patiently, stroking her head gently. When she finally spoke, her voice was trembling.

"I talked to Ben, my brother. Greg, it was really him. He's hurt —and angry. He never got a chance to live. I got everything after he died. He didn't even get to know my parents. I'm sorry, Ben. I'm truly sorry." She pulled away from him and hid her face in her hands. He sat on the edge of the chair and tried to comfort her. She pushed him away.

"Give me a minute. I'll be all right."

While he waited, Greg gingerly fingered the headset and then slowly put it on. The presence was different this time. It was not Oliver.

"I wasn't through talking to her yet. Put her back on. I want to talk to her, not you." The voice was eerie in his head. It had the feeling of a child, yet there was a harshness to it, a cold demanding tone that belonged to an adult. Oliver had been annoying, but this thing was worse, much worse. He snatched off the headset without even bothering to answer the child.

"Let's get out of here," he said. Beth nodded and he helped her back into the kitchen.

"I'm sorry I got so upset. It's all right now." She smiled wanly. "It was Ben, Greg. I'm sure of that."

He thought of the cold voice in his head and almost shuddered. Beth caught his feelings.

"He's not like that," she said. "At least that's not how I remember him. It's just been too hard on him—watching us, seeing me grow up as an only child, taking what he thought was his. It must be hard on all of them. It's part of our vanity. We don't think about life going on without us. But it does, of course, and they have to watch it."

"Is that all they do? Just watch us? Don't they have anything else to do? Why can't they leave us alone?"

She was silent for a moment. "We have to get the Diangelos for Oliver. I promised. He won't let me talk to anyone else unless I get them."

"Fine. Let's not talk to anyone else," Greg said curtly.

"Greg, I have to."

"Beth—" he began, but she interrupted.

"You can't stop me, Greg." Then she turned and left. After a moment, he followed.

He watched Beth closely for the rest of the day. At first she ignored him, then angrily began to exaggerate her actions, waiting for him to catch up with her when she headed toward the back of the house. Once, she sarcastically invited him into the back bathroom with her when, not realizing her destination, he had followed her right to the door. After that, he left her alone. He couldn't prevent her from using the machine. In her own way, she was growing more obsessed than he was.

He retreated to the den and stared blindly at the TV until she came in with dinner. At first he thought it was a peace offering, until he saw a slip of paper on the tray beside the food.

"What is it?" he asked.

"The Diangelos' phone number," Beth said. "I'll call them if you don't want to."

"Where did you get it?"

"Oliver told me," she said.

"Where did he get it?" Greg asked.

"If he can see them, then I guess he can see their phone too," she said.

"Yeah."

She sat beside him on the couch and lay her head on his shoulder. She seemed so tired.

"All right, I'll call the Diangelos," Greg said. "I don't think it's right, but I'll do it."

He waited until she fell asleep and laid her gently on the couch. Grabbing his hat and coat out of the hall closet, he left, not stopping to put them on until he got to the car. He had to get away, to get out of the house and out from under Oliver's eyes.

He drove aimlessly for a while and finally ended up where he had always run to as a child. Down to the Savannah River, to Factor's Walk, where the tourists and the boats paraded by.

It was growing dark and the shops were closing. During the summer there were marching bands and street musicians, but now the walk was almost deserted. The sun had dropped behind the tall waterfront buildings, leaving a dirty grey light on the walk. The tide was high and the Savannah lapped gently against the wooden pilings lining the street.

This was the place for ghosts, he thought, looking up at the dark brick buildings. Some of the structures were quite old, left over from the days of sailing ships and King Cotton. Many of the upper-story windows were boarded up, giving a blind and forbidding feel to the riverfront as the darkness settled in. This was where they told stories of pirates and slaves who still walked the hollow passages connecting the old Cotton Exchange with other buildings. The tunnels were still there—boarded up, but still there.

He walked along the deserted cobblestone street until he found a small hole in the brick wall and put his face to it. Although it was too dark to see what lay beyond, he could feel a cold wind blowing against his face. The moving air meant there were still openings into the tunnels somewhere. As a child, he had never been able to find any entrances, but then, he hadn't really looked. He'd been too afraid of what lived inside. Now that fear seemed insignificant compared to this.

Oliver knew the phone number. Such a simple thing and yet it terrified him. This Oliver was everywhere. He wasn't a creature of the dark, haunting some ancient building. He was here in the daylight, looking at phones and TV sets, always watching.

"You belong in there," Greg said loudly into the hole. There was no echo as the wind swept his words away. He sighed and started back to the car. He'd a hundred times rather face the familiar ghosts of his childhood than this new creature.

Getting the Diangelos down to Savannah was easier than he'd anticipated. He didn't tell Mrs. Diangelo the reason, but he made it clear it was vital. He had forgotten how close they had been to his father. They must have thought Greg was in trouble and Mrs. Diangelo said they'd drive all the way from Atlanta that same day.

Beth spent the day in the shed with her brother. She was uncommunicative when Greg brought her lunch. When he tried to insist she at least pause to eat, she refused and grew angry with him. Finally he left and moved to the front room to wait for the Diangelos. His feeling of uneasiness had changed into outright hate. Maybe it wasn't the machine; maybe it was just Oliver and Ben, but the whole idea seemed wrong. And in the back of his head an idea still nagged, tempting him. But his fear stopped him. Some people were better off dead and buried.

He recognized the Diangelos' car and went outside to greet them. He still hadn't thought of what he would say. As the car pulled into the driveway, Greg saw only one person inside. Mrs. Diangelo was alone. He approached her, shocked at how much she had aged since he had last seen her. It wasn't just her grey hair and wrinkled face; her eyes looked old.

"Greg," she said softly and took his hands. "I haven't seen you in so long."

He smiled uncomfortably. "I don't get out much," he explained.

"You should come and see me. I'd be glad to have you."

"Where's Mr. Diangelo?"

There was an awkward pause. "We're separated," Mrs. Diangelo said. "We'll probably get divorced. It'll be better that way I think, Greg. Now," briskly, she dropped his hands and looked up at him, "what's the problem? Whatever it is, I'll be glad to help."

Shadows 5

Greg stared at the ground, not wanting to meet her eyes. Now he had to tell her. Then Beth appeared, running from the shed.

"Mrs. Diangelo?" she asked. Puzzled, the older woman nodded. "Come here," Beth said. "We've got something to show you." She took the woman's hand and led her to the shack.

"Beth," Greg called after her. This wasn't the way to do it. They mustn't spring it too soon. But Beth was determined and she ignored him. He ran to catch up with her.

Beth took the other woman and sat her in the chair and handed her the headset.

"Beth, don't you think we should explain it first?" he said tensely. Beth ignored him.

"Put this headset on," she instructed Mrs. Diangelo. "It's like a telephone of sorts or a longwave radio. You'll see when you put it on. There's someone at the other end who wants to talk to you."

Greg reached out and grabbed Beth's arm. "No," he said. "You can't give it to her just like that."

"He wants her," Beth whispered fiercely. "You can't stop it."

Greg turned back and looked at Mrs. Diangelo.

"It's all right, Greg," she said softly and put it on. Her eyes went vacant immediately, yet her body grew tense. Greg put his hand on her shoulder, though he knew she couldn't feel it. He wanted to stay, but Beth pushed him out the door.

"Leave her alone. He wants to talk to her alone," she said.

"But shouldn't we stay just in case something happens?"

"No, he doesn't want us to."

"Listen," Greg said angrily, "he doesn't dictate my life. He's a goddamned ghost." He shook her hand off his arm and walked back into the shed.

Mrs. Diangelo was just as he had left her. He watched her closely, but her breathing seemed to be steady. He sat on the worktable and stared out the window at the house, hoping that Beth would come back and apologize. She did not and finally he returned to the house.

She was in the bedroom, lying on the bed. He stood in the doorway and debated whether or not to start the argument again.

"I'm sorry," he said.

"I know." Beth sighed and held out her hand.

He walked over to the bed and sat down beside her. "I wish I'd never built the damn thing," he said.

"Me too." She sighed again. "But they'll never let it go."

As he lay down beside her, she raised her head to look at him. "Greg, you can tell me it's none of my business if you want, but you haven't mentioned your father. Don't you wonder about him?"

Greg answered slowly. "Yes, I've thought about it. The damn machine pulls me like a magnet, but I'm afraid. He meant so much to me and I suppose I don't want to see him changed."

"It does hurt me to see what's happened to Ben," Beth said. "But I couldn't resist talking to him. I guess the pull is pretty strong from our end too."

"Also," he added, even more softly, "I'm not at all sure that my father wants to talk to me. If he asks for me, then maybe I'll consider it, but otherwise—" He let the sentence trail off, but Beth understood.

"Greg," she moved over to kiss him gently. "He does want to talk to you, I'm sure of that. Maybe he just doesn't know about this."

He smiled gratefully. "Yeah," he said. "Maybe."

"Why don't you just relax. Try to sleep for a while."

He lay on the bed next to her and stared at the ceiling, the sleepless night before finally catching up with him. He was glad that he hadn't had to tell Mrs. Diangelo. He had had no idea what he would have said. He only hoped Oliver would be kind.

He slept for several hours. When he woke, Beth was in the kitchen cooking something. Mrs. Diangelo was with her.

He walked in and Beth turned to look at him. She didn't look very happy and he went immediately to Mrs. Diangelo. She sat motionless in one of the chairs, her head bent down so that he could not see her face. He knelt beside the chair and looked up at her. She had been crying.

"He's not happy with the way things have gone," Mrs. Diangelo whispered. "I suppose I have done things wrong, but I did the best I could. He doesn't seem to understand that. He wasn't here—how could I tell what he wanted?"

She began to sob quietly. Greg looked up at Beth, then awkwardly put his arm around Mrs. Diangelo. Beth came around the
table and began to comfort the weeping woman. Greg moved back
gratefully.

"Of course he wasn't there," Beth said. "He has no idea what
you went through."

"Nor does he care," Greg whispered under his breath. Oliver
had no right to do this. She looked in worse shape now than she
had when Oliver had died.

"What are you going to do?" Beth asked Mrs. Diangelo.

"I'm going home," she said. "I'm going to do what he asked."

"What does he want?" Greg asked quietly, trying to control his
anger.

"He wants me to quit my job and go back to Richard. And
Sandra, his fiancée, do you remember her?" Greg nodded. "He
wants her to leave David."

"But David's her husband now," Greg interrupted.

"She was supposed to marry Oliver."

"But he's dead," Greg shouted. Mrs. Diangelo shrugged helplessly.

"What can I do?" she said. "I promised him. Greg, I have no
choice."

"I know." Greg knelt beside her and touched her hand softly.
He felt his anger draining out of him in the face of her anguish. It
wasn't her fault. She was as helpless before Oliver's demands as
he had been.

"I have to go now." Mrs. Diangelo got up and began to gather
her belongings. Her movements were slow and ponderous. She's
grieving, Greg thought. Just as she had when Oliver had died.
Now she's in mourning all over again for a dead son who's come
back to haunt her.

He held the door as she went out. Then he came back into the
kitchen.

"I'm going to destroy it," he said.

Beth just looked at him. "It's too late," he heard her say softly,
just before he went out the door.

The headset was on the chair and the machine was still on.
Oliver was expecting him.

"She deserved it," he said. "She made a mess of things and I'm going to see that she corrects them."

"What right do you have?" Greg realized that he had shouted out loud as well as in his mind.

"She's my mother."

"Not anymore. You're dead. You've got no more rights."

"Thanks to you, that's all different now," Oliver said. Greg seethed at the smugness in his voice.

"You were listening in the kitchen too, weren't you?"

"And in the bedroom last night," Oliver's voice mocked him.

"How dare you!" Greg said.

"I wasn't the only one, old buddy. There's someone else who wants to talk to you." Trembling, Greg flung the headset to the floor. He stood up and glanced around the shed until he spotted an open toolbox in the back. Upending the box, he rummaged through the scattered tools and selected the sturdiest hammer in the box. Then he returned to face the machine.

"There's someone else who wants to talk to you," Oliver's mocking voice still echoed in his memory. Greg knew who that someone was. All along he had been begging for that message. More than anything else, he needed to know that his father had not rejected him this one last time. He wouldn't talk to him. Just put on the headset long enough to know if it was him.

He placed the headset on his head and he knew right away. It was his father. The same man who had quietly stepped outside one night twelve years before and shot himself.

"I thought you weren't going to talk to me. I thought you hated me," Greg said. He had to know.

There was a sigh and suddenly Greg remembered the tired man who had left. He was always too tired to talk.

"I left because of you, son. Do you understand?"

"No," Greg said simply.

"You wouldn't have gotten anywhere if I'd stayed. I thought that if I was gone, then your mother could find someone else and you'd be better off. So you see, I did it for you. You got the insurance money."

"I didn't want it. I didn't mean for you to go." Greg was whispering, but his father didn't seem to notice. He continued to talk in a monotone.

"You should have done more with what I gave you. I didn't plan for you to use the money to set up a half-hearted repair shop in the middle of nowhere with a girl you're not even married to. I had such high hopes for you."

"Please stop," Greg pleaded. His father ignored him.

"Now you've invented something impressive, but you're planning to destroy it. Well, go ahead. I don't care. But you remember. I died for you. Everything you have I gave you—and it cost me, son. It cost me dearly. You think about that. I want you to remember that—always."

Greg yanked the headset off with trembling hands and laid it on the table. Pain and anger coursed through him and it was several moments before he could bring himself back to reality. Moving very deliberately in an effort to control his raging emotions, he picked up the hammer. Then he allowed his anger to come through, blocking out all thoughts except those of the whining man on the other end of the headset.

"I didn't ask you!" he screamed, smashing at the machine. "It's not my fault. I never asked you to do it."

When Beth opened the door and found him, the machine was in pieces and he was pounding on the pulverized remains of the headset.

"Greg," she said.

He dropped the hammer and leaned against the wall, expecting her to approach him. Instead she huddled next to the door. Finally he gathered enough strength to speak.

"They're gone," he said.

She did not move toward him, but spoke quietly instead. "They're with us, Greg. They'll be with us always now."

"No," he said. "No." He went to her and led her back to the house. She didn't resist, but neither did she respond to him as he put her to bed and then sat down next to her.

He thought of reaching for her, trying to comfort her, but he knew she would not allow it. So he sat quietly and stared away from her at the opposite wall.

"They can't reach us," he said. "I destroyed the machine. They'll leave us alone."

"No," she said simply. "They won't." She was silent for a time and then she spoke again. "I have to go back home," she said. "I promised Ben that I'd try to get our parents back together." Greg thought about trying to talk her out of it, but she stopped him. "I have to."

"I'll sell the house," Greg said. "Get an apartment. We'll get married."

"Okay," she said, and Greg knew then she would leave him. He could think of nothing else to say and so they lay together in the dark, waiting.

Suddenly the phone rang. Greg started and then lay still, but Beth reached for the phone. After a moment she turned toward him and held out the receiver.

"It's for you," she said softly. "Your father wants to talk to you."

Introduction

Phyllis Eisenstein is not as prolific as many would wish her to be, but the stories of her hero Alaric have gained her much-deserved attention when they have appeared both in The Magazine of Fantasy and Science Fiction *and in* Arkham House *and* Dell *collections. Dark Fantasy is not her usual framework, yet her range is such that she embraces it easily.*

DARK WINGS

by Phyllis Eisenstein

The house seemed large and empty now that her parents were dead. And yet it was also so soothingly quiet that Lydia would sometimes just stand in the high-ceilinged dining room and relish the silence. No shrill voice came floating from the upper story, no gravelly, grating one from the oak-paneled study, no orders, demands, advice, admonishments. The electricity was gone from the air, leaving nothing but solitude.

She had dreamed of such peace, dreamed as the years and her youth ebbed away, eroded by a struggle she was too weak to win. Dutiful and self-sacrificing, people had called her—nurse, maid, cook, buffer between her parents and the outside world. But behind her back, she knew, they had clucked their tongues over the poor dried-up spinster. What did they know of the guilts and fears that her parents had instilled in her, of the elaborate net of obligation they had spun about her, till she was bound to them with ties that only death could sever? And death had come at last, like a knight on his pale charger, and borne away two coffins that set her free. Still, people clucked their tongues because Lydia lived much as before, alone in her parents' house, alone in her heart. If anything, she was quieter than ever.

Yet some things had changed for her. She painted a great deal more these days, uninterrupted. She had moved her studio from the basement to the big bedroom upstairs, where the light splashed in from windows on three sides. On fine days she would open those windows and let the sea air wash away the smell of paint. In the evenings she walked by the shore, sharing it with tourists and young lovers, and there were no responsibilities to call her home at any particular time. Some nights she would be there long after the noises of traffic had faded to nothing, till only the bell of a distant buoy remained for company. She hardly thought about anything at those times, only enjoyed the dark and the starlight on the waves, and the blessed, blessed silence.

On one such night she saw the bird for the first time. The moon had risen as she watched, its light splashed like a pale and shimmering highway crossing the restless ocean toward Europe. Like a shadow upon that path, the bird caught her eye, its dark wings limned by silvery radiance. For a moment it glided over the waves, pinions motionless in the still night air, and then it swooped upward and vanished in the darkness.

She stood awhile by the shore, straining her eyes for another glimpse of the creature, hoping it would wheel and make a second pass over the glittering water. It was a hawk of some sort, perhaps even an eagle—size and distance were deceptive out over the ocean, where there were no references to judge by. She wanted it to be an eagle, for they were rare in these parts and protected. She had only seen a live eagle here once before, when she was a small child. But though she waited till the moon was high and shrunken, she saw the bird no more, though perhaps she heard the beat of its wings far above her head. Or perhaps she only heard the cool surf beating at the rocks below her feet. At night by the sea, time, distance, and direction all seemed to muddle together, playing tricks on the eyes, the ears, and the mind.

At home she could not sleep for thinking about the bird, and before dawn she was in the studio by yellow, artificial light, with a fresh canvas and dark acrylic pigments spread over her palette. Swiftly, she recreated the impression of the scene, the silver moon-path, the dark bird an instantaneous silhouette, and all surrounded by an impenetrable black that seemed to suck light away from the hard, sharp stars. Blue-black she used, instead of true black—Prussian blue, that velvety shade so dark that only a careful eye could tell it from black, but warmer somehow, softer, deeper. The sky and the bird, Prussian blue. But when dawn added its radiance to her lamps, she saw that she had not captured the mood of that moment. The canvas was dull and dim. Her dilated pupils had perceived a patch of luminous, ethereal night in a vaster darkness, but the paints had given her only the latter.

Light, she thought, as she cleaned the palette and brushes. Light. But all she could remember was the plumage of the bird, blacker than black under the silver moon.

She slept.

Later in the day she walked down to the shore, earlier than usual. This time she carried binoculars hurriedly purchased in town, and she scanned the seaward sky from north to south, searching for a familiar silhouette. Gulls she saw, gulls in plenty, soaring, swooping for food, perching on rocks. Fat gulls, grey on top and white beneath. But no hawks, no eagles. She turned the binoculars westward toward the rooftops of the town, just visible beyond the intervening trees. She saw flecks that might be pigeons, crows, even sparrows, near and far. Ordinary birds. Nowhere did she see the short head, broad tail, and flared wings that marked her quarry.

She ate a quick dinner and returned to the painting by the waning, rosy glow of dusk. One could not evoke the depths of night, she thought, under a bright sun. She lightened her palette, reworked the moon and sea and even the dark air between them, trying to capture the radiance against which the bird had seemed so intense a shadow. Past midnight she realized that there was a contradiction in her mind, a double image of that instant, in which the sky was bright and dark at the same time. She could feel it, but the painting was only a poor reflection of that feeling, two-dimensional and—by now—muddy. She cleaned the palette and brushes and set the canvas aside against the wall. Stifling a yawn, she mounted a fresh, blank canvas on the easel.

The bird this time, nothing else. She sketched quickly, placing tail and flared pinions, adding details that she *felt* rather than remembered. The light was moonlight of course, but there was no sky, no ocean, only the dark wingspan and the merest suggestion

of curved beak and piercing eye. And when she reached the limits
of both her recollection and her invention, she went downstairs to
the study and looked eagles up in the encyclopedia. She knew now
that it had been an eagle; she wouldn't allow it to be anything else.
The encyclopedia illustrations gave her some inspiration and corrected a few of her assumptions, and she hurried back upstairs to
make adjustments.

By dawnlight again, she viewed her new effort with a critical
eye. She had never painted birds before; at most, they had been
pieces of background in her few landscapes, a brushstroke or two
in the sky. The black eagle showed her lack of familiarity with his
kind; he was naïve and awkward, though bold. If she squinted, she
could see a family resemblance to the bird on the back of a dollar
bill.

At twilight she walked by the shore, searching the darkening
sky for him, staying on till the moon was high, that night and
many after. Night upon night, as the moon waned and the stars
brightened by contrast. Night upon night, in fair weather and foul,
when the waves were slick as glass, when the waves were wild
things clutching for the sky. She waited for another glimpse,
straining at clouds or a late gull or a speck of flotsam on the
water. She waited late, late, and past midnight she returned home
and worked on one or the other of the paintings, striving to re-
create the bird.

She had never gone to town much, less since the deaths of her
parents. Now she had no use for the place at all; she had her groceries delivered and paid her bills by mail. Every scrap of her
spare time was spoken for, by paint or binoculars or the sleep that
she grudgingly allowed herself. Only the postman saw her, dropping off a few bills, catalogues, advertisements a couple of times a
week. And the people who walked by the sea. But the weather was
beginning to grow chilly for both tourists and lovers; soon the
moon waxed full again, and only Lydia stood on the shore to
watch it touch the waves with silver.

She heard the bird now, sometimes—she was sure of that,
though she never saw his broad, dark wings. She heard him beat
the air once, twice, high above her head, and then there was silence as he soared and she stared upward, trying to pierce the

blackness with her human eyes. She thought he could probably see her well enough, eagles' eyes being so much sharper than humans', and she tried to imagine how she must appear to him—her face a pale speck amid the darkness of rocks and scrubby grass. A small thing, earthbound, of no significance to a creature who sailed the dark ocean of air. What would it be like, she wondered, to have wings and look down upon the creatures who could only walk?

The paintings had proliferated by this time. They lined the studio, view after view of the subject she had seen only once. Yet there was a clear image of him in her mind's eye, as if she could reconstruct his whole form from the sound of his wings. His eye, she knew, was golden, like a great amber bead set above the corner of his beak. The beak was dark as his plumage, like polished jet. And to display their true span, the great black pinions would require a canvas larger than any Lydia had ever worked. She contemplated ordering the proper size from Boston, stretching it and preparing it herself. She measured the door of the studio to be sure the finished product could be carried out of the room, and then she made the phone call.

Autumn was waning by the time the painting was well begun. The sea breeze that washed her studio was chill by day now, and gusty, though she still opened the windows to it, and painted wearing an old sweater. When she walked by the shore, she could see scarlet leaves floating among the restless waves. The color of the ocean was changing, too, and the color of the sky; the daytime world was beginning to grey out for winter. Only at night were the changes invisible. At night the buoy still clanged far out on the water and the moon still splashed its shimmering highway to Europe almost at Lydia's feet. At night ebony wings beat the air, and Lydia strained for a glimpse, just a single brief glimpse of the bird that glided somewhere, somewhere, in the vast, unchanging darkness.

The days grew shorter as the chilling wind ruffled the waves to a restive froth, and the nights were long—long for walking by the choppy water, long for painting by lamplight. Lydia slept the whole short day through now, seeing the sun only at dawn and dusk. The bird preferred the night hours, and Lydia had begun to understand that preference. Day was jarring, stark, revealing too

much of reality. Night was kind and soothing, hiding the world's
flaws in velvet. At night Lydia could look into her dimly lit mirror
and see the girl she had once been, the girl whose skin bore no
sign of wrinkling, whose hair was yet untouched by grey, whose
life still lay ahead of her. That girl could walk on the shore and
dream dreams; she could look upon the moonlit highway to
Europe and imagine herself traveling it, light as a feather, eastward, over the horizon.

She finished the painting half a dozen times. At dawn she would
step back from it, cock her head to one side, and nod to herself.
She would clean the brushes and palette carefully, then, and go to
bed satisfied. But when she woke at dusk, the light of the setting
sun showed her flaws, approximations, incompleteness, and she
would eat a quick breakfast and go out to the shore again in
search of her model, and inspiration. Inspiration she would find,
in the clang of the buoy or the whisper of the wind, or the faint
rustle of wingbeats high, high. But the model would not show himself, not even his shadow, and she would return home and work
determinedly through the dark hours until she laid the brushes
aside again come dawn.

Half a dozen times, she finished and slept—and then one blus-
tery sunset found her with nothing left to do.

Not that the painting was perfect. She eyed it critically from
every angle, brushes poised in her fingers, palette in the crook of
her arm. She approached it several times, as if to lay another
stroke upon the canvas, then drew back. The paint was very thick
in some places. But she knew another layer would not make it better. The painting was beyond her ability to improve. She set her
brushes aside and went out to walk.

Lydia understood the limits of her skill. She did not expect the
canvas to be a photographic reproduction of the image in her
mind's eye. She knew she would have to be satisfied with the
faintest hint of the beauty and grace and power of the original.
And down by the shore, in the pale light of the full moon, she had
to weep for her own limitations. She wept, and she shivered a little
because the night was very chill, and her coat was not quite heavy
enough.

High above her head, she heard his wings.

She knew the sound instantly and looked up, straining to pierce the darkness, her tears a chilly patch upon each eye, blurring her vision for a moment. As a blur, she saw him silhouetted against the moon, and then she blinked and brought him into sharp focus. He was poised above the shimmering path that the moon laid down on the surface of the sea, his great wings motionless as he glided lower, lower, almost touching the white-topped waves. An eagle—yes, she had been right all the time, right in every detail, even to the amber eye that glittered with moonlight, glittered as it regarded her.

He swooped toward her, his great dark wings blotting out the moon, the sky, the world. She gazed at him in wonder, in adoration; the painting had not matched his true size, not remotely. He was the grandfather of eagles, she thought—the god of eagles. She felt a great gust of air as he hovered over her a moment. And then, as delicately as she might cradle a kitten, his great talons locked about her waist and hips. Her hair blew wild as his pinions cupped air to rise again, and then her feet floated free of the earth. Upward they soared—upward—and the rushing wind was a tonic to Lydia's soul. She felt light, young, and beautiful as the bird himself. Looking down, she could see the silver moonpath flowing far below.

Eastward they flew. Eastward toward Europe.

As the first rays of sunlight spread out over the ocean, Lydia saw the island. The only land visible from horizon to horizon, it was dominated by a huge mountain and, as they drew closer, she realized that the summit of that mountain was their destination. This did not surprise her; where else, she reasoned, would an eagle rest?

Closer still, and she saw the nest, big as her parents' house, built of bushes and driftwood and spars from sailing ships, some with ropes and tattered canvas still clinging to them. And then, at the last moment, just before her feet touched the soft, shadowed interior of the nest, just before they brushed the lining of feathers torn from the bird's own downy breast, and his mate's, she struggled. Poor dried-up spinster, she struggled—weakly—as she fell toward those small, dark, gaping beaks.

Introduction

Terry L. Parkinson has "done clerical stuff in a hospital, telephone soliciting for a Republican newspaper when I was really desperate a few years back, and folded W. C. Fields T-shirts in a factory." He lives in San Francisco and this is his first professional sale—a story of shadows that may or may not be destroyed by the light.

ESTRELLA

by Terry L. Parkinson

The window curtain is the enemy; she pulls it back slowly. The world comes into view as she moves into the frame her hand has made. Green fog crawls about the yard, occasionally pooling and rising vertically, tornado-fashion, then dissipating down into waves, which break at the front door.

There is the iron gate, insubstantial in the fog. A man-shape slides through the bars.

I am a bird in the center of this fog-bound cage, in the clear eye of the creeping, shifting weather; the eye of my house sees and pulls back.

She pulls a handkerchief from the waistband of her dress; with her free hand she dabs at her wet forehead. Heart racing, she is about to take flight.

She drops the curtain. It floats back into place. In a moment it is still. But, out of hand, the curtain lures her; she must peer through again. Will she see a face on the pane as she lifts the curtain a second time?

The shadow of the pursuer is more clear, an area of uncanny defined dark moving against a confusion of gray light and vague bars. She cannot tell whether the pacing figure is inside the gate or outside. Estrella falls back, the breath knocked out of her. Why did he pick this morning to take shape? She stumbles until the backs of her knees break at the familiar edge of the divan, which coughs dust, receiving her.

The cushions provide temporary solace. Has she locked the gate? Will he come knocking?

Shadows, she decides, have a disconcerting habit of always knocking, of never passing by. She counts the ten strikes of the clock. But no knocking comes. She strains, and hears faint footsteps, human footsteps (two-footed, brisk, then shuffling).

She rises, smoothing the wrinkled blue silk dress, shaking dust from her hair. She plunges down the long dark hall to the kitchen; stops; the light from the front door is changed, a slow darkening. He stands there now; she has pulled too far away, and he is coming after.

She closes her eyes. She wishes hard. Be gone. Another day, maybe, when I'm feeling stronger. But the black of her eyelids are him and she opens her eyes, falling into the kitchen, where the shutters let in a bit of healing light.

She puts a pot of water on the stove, removes a cup of spidery blue porcelain from the cupboard, and sits down to wait. A slat of the chair is broken and her legs become numb and heavy. She wonders if she can get up and check the tea water. In three minutes she has decided she must try. Walking now seems completely magical. But she manages to walk on prickly feet to the stove, where the water is unfinished. She reseats herself, and the teakettle begins its furious internal bubbling; she waits for the shriek of the whistle, irritably.

She blows out the fire. The tea leaves—from an unlettered tin—crumble in her hand. She looks about for the strainer, finds it in the sink—unwashed—but uses it anyway. Tea—even old tea—is cleansing, therefore clean.

The weak tea burns down her throat, chasing the pursuer, which is stuck in her mid-chest wall. He had fallen from her inner eye upon entering the kitchen. A warm line crawls down to her belly. She finishes the tea in a gulp. The residue in the bottom of the cup engenders a thought. What if she has swallowed so hard that the intruder has been taken deeper inside her, where there is plenty of nourishment and he could take root? Shadows are so tricky, when inside. Her stomach coils and knots.

She clutches herself as best she can, cinched tight under the dirty and slippery silk; she kneads her stomach for signs of movement; in the same fashion she examines her breasts. She feels a twitching through the fabric. Jesus, she thinks, have I forgotten something? Am I pregnant? And rushes into the bathroom, the house spinning about her. She gasps for breath, leans over the basin, and vomits. Pale brown water trickles out her nose. She cannot bring up more. She carries the fullness in her belly into the front room, walking with tiny fast steps, lies on the couch and breathes deeply, slowly, trying to trick herself into the experience of birth. She falls asleep instead, facedown in the old velvet.

The room is black as pitch. Where is my left arm? She gropes for it, finds it on a pillow. This is mine. Sits up, but cannot orient herself to space—what is that called? Proprio—something. Stands up. This is a room. A room in whose house? Father's house. Things are coming clear. She stumbles, grabs a table's edge. There appear to be four walls—north, south, east, west. This is my house; I have fallen asleep in one of the rooms. She strains to look through the thick black.

Now I remember. The shadow at the front door. The tea. Something in my throat (a tea leaf?). Silly to have panicked so. She pulls at her damp skirt, which is crumpled about her waist. She finds the lamp table—final proof that she is in the front room—and lights the lamp. The room leaps out at her like an angry yellow dog. The clock cranks up, chimes three times.

She walks to the stairway; at the top a cold blue light gleams through a half-open door. The long sleep has emptied her.

She wonders, as she climbs the stairs, how he will look, who he will be this time, what it is she must do. She rustles down the hall, her skirt improperly pulled down and the left leg exposed like a blue cane.

She sighs, makes an attempt to straighten her hair, and opens the door.

As she finishes, dawn breaks over the house. The morning glow fills the walls with warmth; Estrella strides down the stairs to meet this new caller, who is golden-fingered and waving.

She waits on the last stair while the mailman sorts the mail.

She watches his circular shadow through the curtain, amused that yesterday she had been so terrified of contact. She stares at the door; waits. Wall is warm. Looks at her toes. Feeling nothing in particular, she starts to think. I feel good, although I haven't slept. Haven't slept. A memory cuts through the morning on a cold wind. Father would chastise her for not sleeping through the night. Often she woke him with her gentle sobbing at his bedside. "A man with a blank face stood at the end of my bed. The room filled so full of light I was afraid it would burst. I closed my eyes against the light and, when I opened them, it was dark and the man was gone."

The mailman finishes. Estrella starts at the sound of the letter slapping the floor.

What should I do about the slot? Should I tape it up and let the mail be left in the box? That would require going out onto the porch. The morning sun, who is not always friendly, falls directly on the porch, unobstructed by the hedges.

She feels she has been patient with the hedges, but they have become a nuisance. She obviously could not tape up the slot until they grew higher. They grew very, very slowly, contrary to her will.

She had gone out many times and talked to them in her most even, reasonable voice. Please grow faster so that I can walk about in the day without fear; I am sensitive to the sun, as you are. Surely you understand. The hedges remained obstinate and went about their growing with slow cruelty. Parts of the hedge actually seemed to be dying out, to be opening into the other yards. Soon neighbors would be pouring through with questions and admonitions.

Hedges were humming little animal engines; bees filled their insides. I will drink my tea without honey, as revenge.

The letter lies on the floor, radiant and dangerous. The mailman's dark hand had delivered it, reaching out from the circle of his head. Some, Estrella realizes, trying to see all viewpoints and recapture the feeling of morning, would find it desirable to receive such an attractive envelope, to come down the seductive stairs and find that the world has a message for you. Someone more foolish than I might even run down the stairs to retrieve this invitation to another world; someone might even have been insensible from their night-sleep and trip on the last step, breaking their long eager neck. Black blood, like tar, would stain the carpet, setting off the golden packet.

Lucky the mail didn't drop through until I reached the bottom.

Estrella looks at her feet, which are moving about in unknown ways. Her left big toe has worked its way into a hole in the carpet; she watches abstractly as the hole grows larger and another toe disappears inside.

I'll consider the problem of the hedges some other time, she thinks, and reaches down to pick up the mail.

The envelope is silky and slightly warm. She holds it to the light to read the address, which is rain-smudged—190 Black Mountain Road. As though tipped from the letter, images pour through her. (Blood, she thinks, blood rushes to my head when I bend down and causes this spontaneous recall.) She had asked to see it. The halls were a snaking maze of anonymous doors, each door with a nameplate. She memorized the color of each door, the location of the nameplate, whether the keyholes were peekable or not (most were not), times their inhabitants went in and came out. Only two doors were habitually unlocked, and they were closets. She could never, with only these scraps of information, piece together the secret of the place. "A little girl needn't be too curious about things that don't concern her."

She lowers the letter from the light. Blue rivers of ink turn to black. Her back feels on the verge of slipping out. That is certain; that is real. She could bend over again and let it happen. That would be interesting and perhaps stop the rush of blood to her memory cells. She could lie there paralyzed, like brother after his accident, and be relieved of all responsibility. The envelope had lost its heat. But who would take care of Robert? Who knew how long the paralysis would last? The mind had a lot to do with recovery in these matters. She drops the envelope in a box on the desk marked: BUSINESS MAIL, FATHER, ETC. She date-stamps the envelope, which lies on top of several others; must remember to mail in the deposits of the estate checks. She rolls down the top of the caramel-colored desk, decides against the search for the secret compartment. "You know this desk is very old and has lots of secrets. Aunt Mary showed me a special compartment, but it's as difficult to find as it is to open a Chinese puzzle box." Brother shouldn't have been driving so fast, and none of this would have happened.

Estrella feels a shiver of satisfaction at having resisted the desire to search for the compartment. She recalls the one thunderous morning she considered tearing the desk apart; she smiles, licks her salty metallic-tasting lips, humming her way down the hall to the kitchen. The voice breaks into words every third step. My pitch, she thinks, gets better with age. It's a shame Mother didn't live to see the final flowering of my voice. I could not sing for anyone but Mother.

She hesitates before the kitchen door, hearing a flutter, as though a bird has flown against a window. She waits for the shatter of glass, but nothing comes. Well, I have unfinished business elsewhere; and she shuffles back down the hall. Her numb cold hands explore the familiar patterns of the pressed leather—angel's faces, vines, roses. Nothing new there. Puckerings, like scars on the walls. As she reaches the desk, she stumbles out of her slippers, falls against a sharp edge. She pushes herself away. The desk rocks. She pushes it again; it rocks on four feet, steadies. She smiles.

The impulse to search for the magic drawer rises in her. No, she tells herself as she pulls the rolltop up, then immediately back down, this desk is not mine. I have no right to search. See the big round belly of the desk, it is Father's desk, it is brother's; the desk could stand up and walk; it has four legs; it would split apart.

A man stands before her in the space occupied moments before by the desk. He wears a three-piece suit, takes a step, wears a white lab coat. A blink of the eye, and he sags into a blue-and-white-checked hospital gown, open at the back; the checks are blue horses (she squints), tail to head, galloping around the gown. He collapses to the floor, dead from a pinprick at the lab, dead from contaminated blood. She stands by the bed as his hand falls limply against the metal frame; glassy-eyed, neutral, he leaves her for another. Brother comes and guides her away. He drives her to their house, nestled in swelling green lungs of earth; the great white house is mirrored many times in the distant complex of buildings that crawls down into the valley. Father's memory cells. They pass the iron gate, the guard dogs (flat black with eerie wet noses), and she stares off in longing at the white-tiled buildings, wondering what will happen now that he is gone.

Robert puts her to bed, pats her head, later backs from the room. I will not search for the drawer, she thinks, and turns from the desk. Blood trickles from her hand; a crescent moon incision has been made by her thumbnail. The fences, the guard dogs, the final visitor; you all go to the same place, hanging red and blue from the end of his hook.

The living room is dark, drapes pulled fast; the dull air contains the shape of her heavy wet sleeping. A line of antiseptic smell cuts the room; she ducks under it. Robert is calling. Later, later. She looks to the high dark ceiling and pauses; then collapses, weak and boneless, on the couch. Dreams flicker inside a mouth, blue as sky; she walks in. The child feels helpless, alone on the plane, closed in and yet lost; she wants to convey her panic to the other passengers, but they sit around a table, intently playing cards. She tries to break into the circle; finally, one of them turns to her. He is the man with no face. The plane crashes as she hurries back to her seat, and the metal shell falls away from her; she floats to the ground, landing in a boat in the center of a lake; the wreckage streams through the air like orange flowers thrown, and slides into the deep water. Later, she receives an award for having flown the furthest without a plane. She is a winged creature, with wings neatly pinned back for the ceremony. She accepts the award, thanks six people—three scientists (Father's friends); her father; her brother Robert; and the father of her child, whose name she cannot remember. Later, sitting by the fire, she remembers the man's name. But, as it is the same as several other male family members, she closes the book she is reading and goes to bed.

She wakes up startled and, in the black room, a concentrated dark flies over her; she sits up, looks to the ceiling, eighteen feet above. Robert Jr.'s father. What has happened to her son's father? Her body curls with the effort of remembering, but she can call nothing to mind; instead, she pictures the bluish face of her son, lying between two pillows like a swollen vein. She had given birth to him at Black Mountain Hospital, in a quiet wing cleared out for her by her father. Patronizing nurses had tried to quiet her, but she would not be still. She would take him home and keep him alive in a special room. She could not give him up so easily, deformed and half-strangled but still her son.

She pulls herself from the couch, trying to fight the impulse to go back upstairs, for she knows it is too soon.

In the purple light at the base of the stairs she waits; the worn spot in the carpet is like a pool of tar. Her foot suspends over it, then she jumps and lands on the second step. The front door light accompanies her, even and forceful.

She walks up the stairs, eyes closed, seeing a dark line moving like a steel bar across the flashing inner lights. I wonder who the shadow man is who paces in front of the gate? I wonder if someday I shall go out and see his face?

But shadows do not have faces. She opens her eyes. Her own shadow lengthens before her on the stairs, curls around the upper bannister.

She pushes open the metal door; a blue door of light opens across her, and she is another person; the downstairs Estrella is gone.

The room is a tangle of machinery, wires, tubes—a jungle of another mind. She checks the console for his vital signs, finding them adequate, if a little low. Not enough time has passed since her last visit. There are several equivocal readings, but she discards them as muscle artifact (head movement) and erases them from the memory. She checks the leads, the emergency lock on his wrist.

She bends forward like a praying mantis, her thumb depressing the switch that stops her beloved's blood flow into the life-saving machine.

Hello Father, hello brother, hello son, she says to the room. Who will you be for me today?

Soon he will get up and walk away, and I will be left here, unconstructed.

She cradles the swollen head, startled by the heaviness; she weighs it in her palms and says, "This is you, this is real; see, it strains the muscles there, it has substance." Sick faces are both young and old; she cannot think who he is today.

She stands back. I should let you die, Robert. I should.

Ah, it is Robert, but which Robert?

She disconnects the tube from the machine, puts it to her mouth, and releases the switch. She cranes her head forward; the crash of metal on metal roars in her ears; she swallows the warm blood that the machine pumps into her. Robert is still, bluish, eyes red and afraid; his head moves to the left from the midline, then back again; his paralyzed body fills the entire bed like rolls of cloth.

She swallows one last time, replaces the tube. Robert's left hand falls over the edge, bangs the rail. "Something to say?" she asks. She ignores the livid hand hanging against the bed frame, turns to leave. In her stomach, a sea curls and whispers.

But as she puts her hand through the doorway, she spins around to face him. "Son of a bitch," she says, completing the ritual and, half in shadow half in light, closes the door behind her.

Introduction

Marta Randall lives on the West Coast, has taken over the reins of the acclaimed sf anthology series New Dimensions *and is the author of* Islands, Journey, *and* Dangerous Games, *as well as numerous short stories and novelettes. She works almost exclusively in the realm of science fiction, but when the occasion arises she can be persuaded to exercise her extraordinary writing talents elsewhere. As when she decides that the edge of a shadow doesn't have to be gentle, nor does it have to be soft.*

SINGLES

by Marta Randall

Janet Murphy wedged herself more deeply between the wall and the potted palm, holding her untouched glass of champagne before her. Beyond the plant's sparse, sun-starved fronds, bodies twitched and jerked to the beat of loud music. Pulsing multicolored lights barely lit the room; quick white strobes picked out an arm, a hip, a straining face, an opened mouth, a hand. Bosch, she thought. Bosch set to disco. The dense air reeked of cigarettes and cologne and the occasional tickle of dope. The room rang and shook. Janet wondered if she'd lose her hearing before she lost her mind. Cathy had talked her into this and now Cathy spun and stepped on the floor, her blond curls bouncing. A strobe transformed her pretty face, stretching it, caught, head back, hair twisting, the mouth cruelly open. Janet shuddered and looked away.

"Come on," Cathy had said at dinner, grabbing Janet's hand as the dance was announced. "Just try it, just this once. You'll love it. All you have to do is relax and get into it. Really." She stood, tightening her grip.

"But I don't like—" Janet said, and was herded into the ballroom with the other diners. Now she pressed against the wall, holding the champagne glass like a shield, and hoped that no one spotted her. To be here, assaulted by noise and stink and pulsing darkness, was bad enough; to be an active part of it far worse. A couple bumped into the wall on the far side of the palm and kissed passionately, too busy to notice her. The man put his hands between the woman's jeans-clad legs.

"Margaret," he said, moaning.

"Marilyn," she muttered, and put her arms around his waist.

A palm frond poked Janet's back. She shrugged away from it and looked for a means of escape. The noise softened marginally.

"Get down and boogie!" Evan Baker capered about the small stage and smiled hugely as the music surged. Skin-tight grey pants, burnt-orange shirt open to the belt buckle, jouncing profusion of gold chains, and that idiotic grin. Janet suspected him of being an android—*nobody* could be that consistently cheerful. She wondered if his cheeks ached at the end of the day and imagined him rubbing his face while the grin-wrinkles peeled off. He'd keep them taped to the side of his bathroom mirror, she decided, and put them on fresh each morning. Unless, of course, his wife did it for him. Janet's lips twitched.

"Monica," said the man on the other side of the palm. Janet considered making a suicide dash toward the door and saw herself disappearing under a tangle of arms and legs. She emerged cautiously from the palm. Cathy had disappeared into the flashing darkness. Evan's wife Alice kept guard at the big wooden doors. The sequins on her halter flashed as she bounced in time to the music; she watched the room and its occupants with all the relaxed rapacity of a bird of prey. Janet looked away. The french doors leading to the patio were closer, but these too were guarded, this time by the unattached and horny. Janet thought with angry longing of the half-finished novel waiting in her cabin.

"Marcie," the man said in an excess of passion.

Janet dumped her champagne into the potted palm, squared her shoulders, and marched along the edge of the dance floor. A hand reached for her, fingers hard white, arm invisible. She skipped away and aimed for the french doors, starved for air, hunched her shoulders, tucked her head in, and charged. A large male body blocked the exit. She sidestepped and it moved directly into her path.

"Gotta vomit," she yelled without slowing, and suddenly she was into the cool night outside. She ran across the concrete patio until the far rail slammed against her hips. She put her hands on it and leaned forward, breathing deeply, ignoring the footsteps coming after her.

"Done yet?"

She turned. Lanterns along the edge of the patio cast a pale yellow glow; the man looked vaguely familiar. Her back tensed.

"Great exit," he said. "I've spent the past half hour edging toward the door and you rushed it just like a—like a linebacker." He smiled, offering his hand. "I'm Al Hamilton. You're Janet Murphy, aren't you? Cathy mentioned you this morning."

"Oh. Yes." She shook his hand briefly and let it drop. "She pointed you out before dinner. You play tennis, right?"

"I play at tennis," he demurred. "Cathy's something to keep up with. I danced a few with her and I'm exhausted. Disco isn't quite my style."

Janet finally smiled. "Nor mine. I didn't expect to be rounded up and frog-marched in there." She glanced through the doors. "Any minute now they'll turn on the gas nozzles and it will all be over."

He chuckled. "And we alone are left—can I buy you a drink to celebrate our escape? Please? If you hadn't come charging along, I'd still be back there. My God, all that bouncing flesh." He faked a shudder. "I'm not into bodies, as they say out here. I'm into minds. Look, just one drink. As thanks, okay?" He put his head to one side. "Unless they have the bar staked out, too."

She bit her lip, remembering Cathy's injunction to relax, and nodded dubiously.

"But just one. I want to be up early tomorrow."

"To watch birds? Cathy told me about that." He walked beside her along the patio's edge. "She said she couldn't figure out why you were here."

"I told her, she must have forgotten. It was a mistake." Tiny yellow lights bordered the flagstone path, a double track of sparks in the blackness. Janet put her hands in her pockets.

"Tell me yours and I'll tell you mine," he offered.

She shrugged. "I wanted someplace new to spend my vacation, and the ads for Silver Dunes talked about marshes and beaches and dunes. Good seabird-watching places. I just came a couple of years too late, I guess."

"Too late?"

"Cathy says the Bakers are new management here. There was some sort of unpleasantness ten years ago and the place closed down for a while, then it reopened as a sort of tattered resort and just kept going downhill. The Bakers bought the place a couple of years ago, renovated—this is their first season."

"What sort of unpleasantness?" He had a pleasant voice.

"A string of murders or something, some psychopath killed a lot of single women and dumped them in the marshes. I don't think they ever caught him." She frowned. "Gory stuff. Cathy was all ready to go into detail, but I didn't want to hear about it."

"I don't blame you. Still, ten-year-old murders are hardly news, although that dreadful music is. You could leave."

"Not really. They don't refund deposits and I don't have much mad money, on a secretary's salary. And I haven't seen the marshes yet." She paused. "And you?"

He gestured widely, a swing more felt than seen in the darkness, but didn't try to touch her. "A mistake too, but a dumber one. I just moved to the city six months ago, and I knew San Francisco was a pretty place, but not how lonely it is. I'm not much of a joiner, the other folk at the office are married or attached, I don't feel comfortable in singles' bars, and I'm not gay. Out here, that seems to be a pretty hopeless combination. So I guess I thought that, maybe being around other singles for a couple of weeks, I'd find some, well, companionship. Someone to talk to. I didn't know I was signing up for compulsory hot tubs and mandatory disco."

She laughed, relaxing. "Yes, I know. But with a little planning you can probably avoid the peacock-feather stuff."

Light and voices spilled from the bar and over the umbrella-sheltered tables on the patio. Janet bit her lip again, unwilling to go inside.

"Tell you what," Al said quickly. "I'll get us something and we can sit out here."

He's not a maniac and I'm supposed to relax, she reminded herself firmly. "Fine. A gin and tonic."

"Got it."

She slid into a chair as he hurried away. The late-spring air was cool and smelled of the sea; beyond the faint thumps from the ballroom she heard the cry of a marsh owl. The patio lights were off; overhead a few stars glimmered from the dark branches of trees. Al pushed open the door with his shoulder and came across to her, holding a drink in each hand.

"Met up with General Alice." She smiled and took her drink. "Had to pretend I had a hot date in the bushes. My God, do you think that woman owns the local contraceptive concession?"

"No. She's probably just got a rather horizontal concept of happiness."

Al laughed. He'd blend right in with the Montgomery Street troops, she thought. Light hair fashionably long, neatly dressed, clean shaven. But his smile was easy and his manner relaxed, and he did appear to have a brain. She decided that she approved of Cathy's taste in men and that made it all perfectly safe; if he was Cathy's, he was as unavailable as Janet herself. He put his glass down.

"I may live after all," he announced. "You're a secretary? What kind?"

"Glorified. I manage a law office."

"Sounds interesting."

"It's not, but it is secure. I spend most of my time stone bored, but that's the breaks. You?"

"Oh, brokerage firm. I get up early and work late, and the firm keeps me traveling around. Atlanta, Houston, Seattle, and now San Francisco. Don't you find it lonely? The city, I mean?"

"No." She wasn't going to elaborate, but saw his raised eyebrows and smiled. "I'm the oldest of seven children," she said, "and I raised them all, more's the pity. It's given me a long-lasting respect for peace, quiet, and solitude."

"And a grave disrespect for disco."

"That it has." She finished her drink.

"Another?"

"No, thanks. I want to be on the beach by dawn."

"May I walk you to your cabin, then?" He put his hand up quickly, palm out. "I won't bite. I promise. It took me years to work up enough courage to shake hands on the first date."

She shrugged and let him walk beside her, listening to him talk about California weather, his first earthquake, the taste of real sourdough french bread. And, standing in the puddle of yellow light before her cabin, he shook her hand, thanked her, and turned to leave. She bit her lip.

"Al." He turned in place. "Would you—are you interested in birds at all? You could come with me tomorrow, if you like."

He grinned. "I'd love to. You can watch birds and I can protect you from psychopaths."

She smiled back. "It'll be early—"

"For a stockbroker on the West Coast, nothing's too early. Dawn? Crack of?"

"Five-thirty, in the kitchens? Someone can fix us breakfast."

"I don't eat breakfast," he said. "I know, it's a reprehensible habit and I'll die of it at an early age. Pick you up at the kitchen instead, at about six?"

"Six it is."

"Great." He waved and went away.

She stepped inside, locked the door, and smiled. Easy to listen to, easy to talk to—and Cathy was interested in him, she remembered. "A real hunk," Cathy had said. "Good moves, good mouth; I can hardly wait to get my hands on him." Janet found that slightly predacious, but perhaps the girl did have some solid interest in Al. And after all, Janet hadn't come to Silver Dunes for romance. Messy, uncomfortable stuff, romance; miserable alone and dangerous if reciprocated. She'd talk to Cathy about it; if Cathy objected to a bird-watching morning, Janet could just as easily let it slide. She changed into nightgown and robe and sat before the fireplace with her book, listening for Cathy's footsteps in the cabin next door.

Janet woke at midnight, cramped and chilly. Cathy's cabin was silent and dark. Janet closed the curtains again and stumbled off to bed.

"Over there," she whispered, pointing into the white morning. "Pelican."

The grave brown bird looked like a pterodactyl. It hovered over the waves, dove, and emerged soon after, pouch empty and expression glum. Janet raised herself on her elbows. "Watch this."

The bird peered suspiciously at the waves, raised its long-beaked head, and took off, wings pounding and legs paddling frantically on the water. Once airborne, it strove mightily for dignity again. They laughed, watching it. Janet lowered her binoculars. A high fog bleached away the day's colors; the Pacific looked big and cold and grey, and Janet watched it with appreciation.

"You really love this, don't you?" Al said.

"Yes." She put the binoculars away. "I grew up outside of Atwater. You've never heard of it; it's a small town in the San Joaquin Valley." She tugged at the sleeves of her jacket and smiled at him, comfortable and unwilling to wonder why. "Flat and boring and dull. By the time I left high school, Dad had a good job and my mother could stay home with the younger kids, so I lit out for the ocean."

"San Francisco? College?"

"Both. Worked nights, studied days, got a master's in history, and discovered there weren't any jobs. And went to work as a secretary."

"You could have gone into orthi—ornth—"

"Ornithology? No jobs there, either." She brushed a strand of brown hair from her forehead. "Any more interrogatories, your honor?"

Al grinned. "Millions of them. I like to pick people's minds."

"Do you? It's your turn now, Mr. Hamilton. Tell the court all about it."

He groaned and twisted to sit beside her, staring as she had done out to sea.

"City boy, born and bred. New York. Grew up there, went to school there, got a job there, got married there, got divorced there, got out of there, and here I am."

"Married?"

"At twenty-one. It was a mistake, but we kept at it for three years. No kids, thank God. You?"

She shook her head. "It never seemed appropriate. Peace and quiet and solitude."

"You've never even lived with anyone?"

"Not that way, no." He looked surprised. "Never wanted to. I don't even have a roommate now, I just prefer living alone."

"No wonder it's impossible to find good women in the Bay Area. You're all in hiding."

"Not entirely. And the theory I hear most is that all the good men are either married or gay."

"Janet," he said gravely, "there seems to be a serious error in communication here." He reached for her. She jumped up, grabbed her binocular case and field guide, and marched down the dune. He scrambled after her.

"Janet, wait. Please." He took her arm and swung her around. She shook his hand away. "I'm sorry. I didn't mean to—hell, I did mean to, but I didn't mean to jump you. Please?"

Her anger faded marginally. "I'm sorry too, Al. I don't like being grabbed—I *hate* being grabbed." She stuffed the field guide into her pocket. "I thought you were different."

He spread his hands. "I am different. I like you. I like women who think. I like attractive women who think. I don't generally grab—I guess I'm more desperate than I thought."

"Lovely." She started toward the trail head. "Desperation makes the heart grow fonder."

"Please." He fell into step beside her. "You're awfully sensitive, aren't you?"

"Nonsense. I'm realistic," she said coldly. "I don't believe in fairies or vampires or little green men or love at first sight or living happily ever after. You put one foot in front of the other and keep your eye out for potholes, and if you're lucky, you come out the other end with relatively few wounds. And that's the best you can hope for."

Al was silent for a moment. "That's not too damned much, is it?" he said finally.

"It's sufficient."

"Sufficient. And where does imagination fit into that? Or love?"

"They don't."

They made the rest of the walk in silence.

It wasn't really Al, she told herself later as she lay in the bathtub, trying to conquer feelings of angry disappointment. Companionship, attractive women who think—it was a line, no more, and her fault for almost falling for it. A sparrow chittered from a bush outside and steam coated the window. Sweet words and promises, and what did it come down to, finally? Helen, back in high school, dead of a botched abortion. Bette, dropping out of college to put her husband through medical school, now divorced at thirty-two with three children, working temporary jobs to keep the family together. All the marriages that disintegrated and the relationships that disappeared, women losing careers to men or men to careers, and all too often losing both. Sitting on the stools at singles' bars on a Friday or Saturday night, wondering how they'd pay the babysitter and trying not to look desperate. Janet watched them from the background and decided early on to travel fast and travel alone, keeping the world at arm's length, safely away. It may not have been the life she dreamed of at seventeen, she thought as the bathwater drained away, but she had survived. Many had not. She pulled on a clean pair of jeans and a fresh shirt. Al Hamilton wanted to be friends—very well, they could be friends. Very distant friends. Ignoring the disappointed hollow in her chest, she tied a scarf around her wet hair, picked a book, and took it with her to lunch.

Neither Cathy nor Al were present. Janet propped her book against the breadbasket and began reading and eating, ignoring the other diners until Alice Baker slid into the seat across from her. Janet closed her book and raised her eyebrows.

"You're Janet Murphy, aren't you?" Alice touched her red hair with carefully manicured fingertips. "I really don't get to know our guests as well as I should, but we do give it our best shot, absolutely." She smiled uneasily and Janet glanced over her shoulder. Evan's place at the front table was empty, the plates clean. "Are you enjoying Silver Dunes?" Alice said as though by rote.

"Very pleasant," Janet lied diplomatically. "Perhaps, though, if you didn't make some activities so—compulsory?"

"Well, I'll certainly look into that." Alice twisted the tablecloth around her fingers. "Have you seen Cathy Gordon today?"

"Cathy? No. Why?"

"You usually eat with her, don't you?"

"I was on the beach this morning and missed breakfast. Is something wrong?"

"Oh no, not at all." Alice smiled warmly. "I just noticed that she wasn't around this morning. Lovely girl, isn't she?" Alice pushed her chair away and stood. "Well, thanks so much," she said, already looking around the room. "And we'll consider your recommendations; I'm sure they'll be so helpful." Janet watched her walk away. No Cathy, no Al, no Evan Baker. Perhaps he'd misplaced his grin-wrinkles, she thought meanly, and was busy hunting for them. She went back to her book.

She strolled by the pool after lunch—and by the tennis courts—but Cathy wasn't at either of them. Nor did she answer when Janet knocked on her door. She frowned, drumming her fingertips on her thigh. Cathy was such a child. Mid-twenties, pretty, gregarious, intelligent, self-involved. She'd probably gone to one of the other beaches, or into town. Wherever she was, she wouldn't be alone. Cathy's chatter of ancient murder had gotten to her, Janet thought angrily. There were no psychopaths at Silver Dunes, except whoever picked the music, and no reason to be worried. But instead of changing into her hiking boots and going to the marsh, she pulled on her bathing suit. Intuition and hunches were both just superstition, but Cathy's absence bothered her, and the bother wouldn't go away. One day away from the birds wouldn't make that much difference. Besides, the pool lay between the main buildings and the cabins, so she'd spot Cathy as soon as the girl showed up. Partially reconciled, Janet spread her towel over a chaise lounge and covered her legs with tanning lotion. The fog rode high above the trees, but its white light was deceptive; one could still burn. Bikinied bodies of both genders lay attractively displayed around the pool. Janet sniffed and lifted her book.

A few minutes later Al Hamilton pulled up a chair and sat, smiling tentatively at her. To her vast annoyance, her chest tightened.

"No birds this afternoon?"

"No." She put the book down, deliberately casual. "Have you seen Cathy around?"

He shook his head. "But from what I hear, she was dancing pretty close to Evan Baker last night. Maybe they—" He gestured vaguely. Janet nodded, feeling sorry for Alice. This probably happened all the time; it would be Evan's fault for encouraging it. "I'll bet they both show up for dinner," Al said.

"Probably." She looked at his sandals. "No tennis?"

He spread his hands. "Well, no. I'd rather join you, but . . . Hell, Janet, everytime there's something I really—am interested in, I screw it up." He made a face. "I am sorry about this morning. I feel like an ass."

She smiled. "Forget it, Al. Maybe I was a bit abrupt, too. Come on, get your suit and I'll buy you a beer."

He grinned, transforming his face. "Make it a Perrier and you've got a deal," he said, rising. Janet turned to flag down a waiter.

Within half an hour she stopped making excuses and simply enjoyed his company. They lay near each other on the lounges and made up histories for the other bathers, each story more scurrilous than the last. Al imitated a cable car gripman driven to wit's end by a load of tourists. They joined a game of tag in the water and she forgot about Cathy and marsh birds and her own soapy promises in the bathtub before lunch. In the laughter and motion of the game she even forgot to jerk away from the occasional touch of Al's body against her own. And, finally, they lay side by side in the waning sunlight, silently watching each other's eyes.

"I like you, Janet Murphy," he whispered. She closed her eyes, hearing it as a promise. "God, it's late. I've got to call the office." He pulled his watch from his shirt pocket, looked at it, and groaned. "Damn. See you later?"

"Sure."

He bent suddenly and touched her eyelids with his lips, so quickly that she had no time to pull away. He walked away and she put her fingertip to her eye. Something in his kiss had felt cold, a little hard, like a fingernail. A tooth, she thought sleepily, and the sensation faded. She lay still a moment longer, then stood briskly, wrapped her towel around her waist, collected book, lotion, and sunglasses. Nitwit, she told herself without emphasis. Her lips tingled.

A few minutes before dinner he called to say he was still tangled in office business but would join her later. Feeling disappointed, she knocked on Cathy's door. No answer. The afternoon's formless anxiety returned. She tightened her lips and went into the dining room.

Cathy wasn't at dinner either, but Evan was. He wore tight forest-green pants, a patterned silk shirt, and an expression caught between self-satisfaction and contrition. Alice, beside him, looked grim and a young brunette at a nearby table kept stealing longing glances at Evan. Janet drew some obvious conclusions, but if Cathy hadn't been with Evan, where was she? Janet pushed food around her plate, pretending to listen to the young man across from her as he nattered on about est and jogging. Content free conversation. She stood.

"Be right back," she told the young man and went out of the room and down the hall to the registration desk. She tapped on the bell until the evening clerk appeared.

"I want to know if a friend has checked out," she said. "Cathy Gordon, Cabin A-5."

The clerk consulted the register. "No, she's paid through until Saturday."

"That's what I thought. Listen, I promised to leave some books in her car, but I've forgotten the license number. Could you . . ."

"Sure. Here it is; green Mustang, 859 SCN. Should be in the lot out front."

"Thanks." Janet left a dollar on the desk and ducked out the main doors into the parking lot.

Floodlights lit the main gate, but left the parking lot in darkness. Janet started down the first row, wishing for a flashlight and peering at license plates. When she arrived at her own car, she took the flash from the glove compartment and went through the lot again, but Cathy's car wasn't there. She returned the flashlight to her car. It can't happen here, an annoying little voice sang in her head. The Zebra Killers took potshots at San Francisco pedestrians; the Trailside Killer murdered women in the parks . . . she banished all the terrifying names impatiently. I'll get as bad as an old woman, she thought angrily as she returned to the lodge. Burglars in the shower and rapists in the closet and everyone on the street a sniper or a mugger or—I don't need this. Cathy's a grown woman, no idiot; she can take care of herself. She's safe. No reason to assume that, just because she's been gone for a while, that she's been—she pushed that thought away, too, and slid into her seat just as the waiter came with coffee.

"Thought you'd skipped out on me," the young man said.

Janet smiled. "You know how it is."

"I hear you."

Her mouth twitched. "Any idea what they've got planned for tonight?"

"Band in the bar and lifeguard at the pool. You wanna boogie?"

"No, thanks, I'm a Virgo," she said with a straight face, finished her coffee, and left. She called Al from her cabin, but his phone rang, unanswered, while she inspected the lock on her door. She put down the phone and consulted the memory of Hangman Brown, one of the firm's more colorful clients, currently doing fifteen years in San Quentin for burglary. She removed a credit card from her wallet, experimented with it, and a few minutes later stood in the tiny front room of Cathy's cabin.

Cathy's cosmetics and hair dryer littered the counter in the bathroom. Her miniscule bikini hung over a towel bar and her clothes were draped in cheerful disorder around the room. Her purse lay open by the dresser. Janet went through it quickly, finding Cathy's wallet but not her car keys. She frowned—it didn't seem right. She left everything as she'd found it and returned to her own cabin, where she pulled on a sweater and put her keys and wallet in her pocket. Then she went in search of Alice and Evan Baker.

Evan gyrated on the small dance floor in the bar, surrounded by women. Alice greeted Janet with a professional counselor's smile and readily agreed to a stroll. "I'm never too busy for a little chat," she said, following Janet outside. They walked across the patio toward the lawn. Most of the tables were occupied; Janet kept walking until they were alone.

"Cathy Gordon's still missing," she said. "I don't like it. I think we should search for her, or at least call the sheriff. There's a fair amount of undeveloped country around here; she could be lost or in an accident."

"Search?" Alice said. "Why? She's probably just off with one of

the young men; you know how it is." Alice smiled broadly.
"They'll be back before breakfast."

"Who is she with? Who else is missing?"

Alice laughed. "Janet, there are sixty-two people here, not
counting staff. I can't keep track of each of them. Come on, you're
on vacation. Relax a little. Spend some more time with that nice
man you've been with. I'm sure your little friend is fine."

Janet clenched her teeth. "Don't you give a damn whether—"

"Anger won't solve anything," Alice said sharply. "Cathy Gordon is a self-centered little girl who'll sleep with anyone and that's
probably what she's doing right now. She'll show up tomorrow,
wondering what all the fuss is about." Alice spread her hands.
"I'm just trying to be moderate. If Cathy hasn't shown up by mid-
morning, I'll call the sheriff. Okay?"

"Right, when it's too late," Janet said bitterly. "What do you
have against her, anyway? Just that you thought she spent the
night with your husband?"

Alice glared. "That was childish and unnecessary, and quite un-
true. You just have to understand my position, too. Evan and I
are new here. We're trying to make Silver Dunes into something
big. We've put in a lot of time and money, and I'd hate to see one
unfounded rumor ruin the entire thing."

"There's no unfounded rumor. Cathy has disappeared. Or
maybe you don't care how many people get hurt, as long as you
make your profit."

The corners of Alice's mouth went white. "You've been doing
your homework, haven't you?" she whispered urgently. "You
don't have to talk about it, you know. We'll do everything we can
for Cathy, but you don't have to mention it to anyone. Just give us
a chance. It really doesn't have anything to do with us, anyway.
It's not our fault and it's not fair that—"

"My God, Alice," Janet said. "You don't mean that bunch of
murders ten years ago, do you? What possible harm—"

But Alice's eyes widened and she put her hand to her mouth,
turned abruptly, and strode toward the bar. Janet gasped and ran
after her.

"You didn't mean those, did you?" she demanded. "There's
something else." Alice shook her arm away. "Damn it, Cathy's

not the first, is she? There've been others, and you're covering it up, and—"

"Leave me alone!" Alice shouted, broke away, and ran around the corner of the building. Janet turned quickly toward the parking lot.

"Janet!" Al strode across the lamp-lit patio. "I'm sorry. Those idiots at the office can't do a damned thing by themselves and I spent the past two hours—"

She grabbed his hand. "I think Cathy's in trouble—big trouble—and I've got to find her." She outlined Cathy's absence, her missing car and keys, Alice Baker's refusal to help. "And Cathy's not the first, Al. Alice as much as said so, but she's hiding it. There have been others."

"Another psychopath? I don't believe it."

"I don't care!" She closed her eyes and took a deep breath. "Even if she's just been in an accident—I know she's in her car, or near it—I've got to look for her, Al. I know she needs help."

"I'll come, then. I'd hate to lose you, too."

She squeezed his hand, relieved, and led the way to the parking lot. Her battered Toyota started, for once, without protest. Al buckled his seat belt as she flicked on the headlights and drove out of the lot.

"First toward the beach." Al nodded. She lowered her window and drove slowly, peering at the low brush and the ditch beside the road. Al leaned from the passenger-side window.

"Nothing," he said when they reached the small parking area by the beach where the road dead-ended. The parking lot was deserted. Janet turned the car around. At least the road ran inland here, not along the cliffs as did Highway 1 for most of its length. If they had to search the coast road too . . .

She drove by the resort gate, peering at her side of the road. The land dipped and the road entered a small stand of eucalyptus and oleander bordering the marsh. Janet squinted, trying to see through the underbrush. A barbed wire fence ended in a tangle of vines; some of them—and the bushes a few meters away—looked bruised. She stopped the car and put it into reverse.

"What do you see?" Al looked at her side of the road.

"Over there, it looks like . . ." She stopped the car on the shoulder and peered across the road. "It is, Al. Something's been through there. Can you see the tracks?"

"I don't—oh, by the big tree? They could be pretty old."

"Maybe." She killed the engine and hauled on the parking brake. "I'm going to take a look."

"Janet, it's dark. God knows what's out there. Let's go back and call the sheriff—and to hell with Alice Baker."

"No. If Cathy's in there, she probably needs help. Come on, I've walked night marshes for years. There's nothing to be afraid of."

She took the flashlight from the glove compartment and slammed her door, letting the beam of light play on the ground as she crossed the road and walked toward the oleanders. Al walked behind her and slightly to the side, peering over her shoulder at the ground.

The tire prints were sharp and clean of any fallen leaves or mud. A patch on the eucalyptus caught the light, strips of bark torn away to expose the shiny underwood, just where a car's bumper would hit it.

"There," she said.

Al took her hand. "I see it. Let me take the lead. It might be dangerous."

"Don't be silly." She marched ahead, both annoyed and comforted by his solicitude. She reached her hand back and he laced his fingers through hers, coming up to walk beside her. The trees fell away behind them; ahead the land dropped abruptly into the marsh, and the tire prints ran straight and clean toward the overhang. Janet stood on the lip of the drop and raised the flashlight. Cathy's green Mustang rested unevenly in the marsh below, its right headlight almost buried. The car windows were dark. Janet's skin went cold under the warmth of her sweater.

"My God." She dropped Al's hand abruptly and slid down the wet hill. The beam of the flashlight danced crazily.

"Janet! Wait!"

Viscous water filled her shoes and lapped at her ankles, slowing her. Al caught up with her and took her hand. She shook it free.

"Cathy! Cathy, can you hear me? *Cathy!*"

Even the marsh birds were silent. Janet cursed the uneven footing and tried to keep the light steady on the car's rear window.

"Janet, you'll break your neck." Al pulled her to a stop. "You can't help her if you're hurt yourself. Slow down."

She leaned against him, trying to catch her breath. His heartbeat was slow and steady and strong. Then she stood away from him and together they slogged to the car. Janet put her hand on the rear fender. Dirty water had splashed over the windows as the car fell; she couldn't see in through the mud. Al took the flashlight from her, moved to the driver's door, and opened it.

"Al? Is she . . ."

He gestured and looked away. Janet's throat tightened. She splashed toward him and he wordlessly handed her the flashlight.

"Cathy?" she whispered.

Cathy's forehead rested against the steering wheel, her long blond hair hiding her face. The strands near her cheeks looked slick and dark. One hand, palm up, lay relaxed on the seat by her thigh.

"Janet, come away," Al said. "Let's call the sheriff. This can't help."

She heard the words distantly and they seemed to have no meaning. Her hand rose, almost without her volition, and touched Cathy's cold shoulder, then Janet tightened her grip and pulled the girl away from the steering wheel. Her bangs were dark with blood, but her forehead was smooth and unbroken.

"Janet, please."

Her fingers brushed Cathy's stiff hair, pulling it away from her temples and cheeks. Such a pretty, flighty, innocent child . . . Cathy's face was serene, smoothly youthful; her lips tilted in a slight smile. And where her left eye had been there was a hole, a smooth emptiness that swallowed the light of the flash as though it went back forever and ever, all the way to the back of Cathy's skull. There was nothing in Cathy's head, save the diffuse beam of light. Nothing within at all.

Janet dropped the flashlight and stepped away shakily, unable to scream. She stumbled into Al's body and he put his arms around her, holding her tight.

"Hush. It's all right, baby. It's all right." He turned her around in his arms and she buried her head against his shoulder.

"I don't understand—Al, how could—what did—" She shuddered convulsively in his arms, seeing Cathy's serene face and the hideous darkness where her eye had been. "After," she said, fighting against sobs. "It must have been—after. She didn't know about it— she was smiling—she couldn't have—Christ, Al," she screamed, "what was it? What did that to her? What kind of—of monster ate her brain?"

"A careful one, I'd guess," he said easily. "And a very, very fast one." She jerked away from him in shock. Al smiled, hands at his sides, his eyes bright in the darkness. Janet stumbled backward.

"A gentle sort of monster, who likes leaving smiles behind." Something flickered between his lips, pale and cylindrical and hard. She backed against the car, remembering the feel of his lips on her eyelids.

"This isn't funny," she said shakily. Her foot hit the flashlight.

"It's not meant to be." The pale something appeared again, framed in Al's smile. He stepped toward her and she grabbed the flashlight. "Come, Janet, you're an intelligent woman. You can understand a gentle monster, can't you? One who doesn't like to fight?"

She jumped to her left. As he lunged, she turned and slammed the flashlight against his temple. He staggered. She scrambled across the hood of the car, tilting it into the marsh; Cathy's body toppled from the seat. Janet leaped from the car and tried to run. The marsh sucked at her. Al Hamilton laughed.

"Marsh walker," he cried derisively. Janet struggled frantically toward higher ground. He was heavier; he'd sink deeper; it would slow him down—she clawed at the bank, the flashlight tight in her hand, fighting against the pull of the marsh, the mud, the slope. She gasped and the marsh released her; she reached for a twisted root overhead and Al's hand closed around her ankle, pulled her back, twisted her onto her back. He knocked the flashlight away and dropped his body onto hers, pinning her to the mud. She twisted her head wildly, trying to escape his eyes and his smile and the terrible thing between his teeth.

"A monster, Janet?" he said in his pleasant voice. "I haven't hurt you. I've never hurt a single one, and I'm very, very good at this." His hands pressed her cheeks and temples, stilling her. He chuckled softly and lowered his head toward hers.

"And I do love women who think."

Introduction

Beverly Evans returns with something quite a bit different than her previous "Waiting for the Knight." Like many dark fantasies, this began with an actual incident. How it ends, however, is something we won't even begin to speculate on.

THE PIANO MAN

by Beverly Evans

The piano was almost hidden in the rear of the music store, back behind the "family" organs and racks of returned rental instruments, each one mottled from the sticky sweat of children's fingers. The keyboard had been removed, and the dusty padding beneath was matted and ridged in regular intervals. The oak finish was original, and so fragile that a casual thumbnail could flake it away like chips of mica. The piano seemed to smile across the store, its wide, toothless, cotton-felt gums bared in a steady, strangely compelling expression.

Katie Prescott stood at the entrance of the music store and stared back at the piano. Years of memories welled up inside her; memories of hours spent practicing, memorizing, sometimes crying, eternally practicing; of little black dots buzzing before her eyes, swarming like so many no-see-ums on a hot summer day; of her first recital, with new anklets, new white sandals, a fresh Tonette, and all the confidence of a four-year-old capable of conquering the world . . . and the laughter. Waves of laughter that went on interminably as she had had to pull her long polished-cotton gown up around her waist in order to climb the high piano stool. The people had laughed, *how* they had laughed at the tiny blond child and her awkward, chubby little legs and her ruffled Carter's undies. Somewhere in her desk at home, a yellowed newspaper clipping from the Atlanta *Herald*, dated August 1952, still silently proclaimed: "Prodigy Bares All In First Recital."

"It's a beauty, isn't it," the music store's salesman said.

Katie started. "Oh yes . . . yes, it is . . ."

"Just came in yesterday. We sent the keys out for new ivory . . ."

Katie couldn't stop staring at the piano. She remembered playing her repertoire of nursery rhymes and sonatinas flawlessly, while hot tears of humiliation ran down her cheeks and made damp stains on the lap of her gown. Katie threaded her way through the weekend shoppers and ran a finger across the curved keyboard cover. The feel of it sent little shivers through her, and she wiped the minute flecks of varnish from her fingers onto the leg of her jeans. LUCHENBACH, GRAND CABINET was still visible in carefully hand-painted gold lettering.

The salesman prattled on, "An old guy called in, asking to handle the repairs on this one. We don't usually contract out privately, but he was so insistent, we gave him the job. . . ."

Fourteen long years, Katie thought as she looked over the Luchenbach; fourteen years since she had touched a piano, much less played one. She remembered her mother screaming, shouting horrible, unforgivable things at her the day she left home, the day Katie had announced that she couldn't take one more minute of living like the only inmate in a prima donna's prison. Up at five to practice before going to school. Home immediately to practice until dinner, then another hour of practice before homework . . . eight hours a day on weekends . . . and the recitals, the intense competition, year after year . . .

"How much?" Katie heard herself ask the salesman.

"Four twenty-five, including delivery and the first tuning in your home."

Snatches of old nightmares whispered at her: losing her place during a performance; the huge wooden church doors closing on her hands, crushing her fingers forever; the old fear of being tied to the piano bench until her hour was up . . .

Katie touched the piano carefully, as if it were alive. She felt a longing—an ache—and a revulsion. She wanted this piano, and she couldn't have begun to explain why.

"Can I leave a deposit?" she fairly whispered, her throat suddenly dry.

"No problem. Why don't you step over . . ."

"Will twenty dollars be enough?" she interrupted.

"That'll be just fine. And your name?"

"Prescott. Katie. Miss."

Katie brushed a wisp of blond hair out of her eyes and looked at the office clock for the third time in five minutes. Only three-thirty. She groaned silently, and turned her concentration once more to the stack of invoices on her desk. Even after five years of bookkeeping for Weston and Smith Manufacturing, the end-of-the-month closing statements still made her irritable and impatient. But today it was something more.

Her Luchenbach had arrived at her home in Marathon in less than a week, and Katie was glad to be set apart from her neighbors by large-acre lots. The piano was horribly out of tune. The notes were so sour that she winced just trying to limber up with some simple scales. Some of the keys were sticky; the ivories overlapped the black keys and caught on the edges; the sound-board was cracked and the buzz was noticeable, but not too distracting. When the piano had arrived, the pedals were disconnected, but she had remedied that with a rubber washer and a common nail.

But today the tuner was coming and Katie caught herself humming stanzas of Chopin and Mozart with pleased anticipation.

Four-thirty came and Katie raced up I-81, keeping a cautious watch for radar traps. Once at home, she found she couldn't sit still, so she changed into her jeans and T-shirt and tackled the broken front door bell—a chore that had cropped up on her weekly "must-do" list ever since she moved in three years ago. A white picket fence, the border of petunias and marigolds running to the front step, the trellis alive with morning glory and honey-suckle, the massive oak spread protectively over one side of the roof. FOR LEASE OR RENT the sign had said. Katie did neither. Instead she put up her entire savings for a down payment on the vacant little farmhouse, purchased a *Handyman's Hints* from the local True Value hardware store, and spent her spare time plastering walls, restoring woodwork, and earning every blister on the hands that she used to treat with such care.

Katie was on the front porch, busy with pliers and screwdriver, when a soft voice from the sidewalk brought her upright.

"Miss Prescott? I'm the piano man—or what's left of him."

He stood on the sidewalk, case of tuning tools in one hand, a white-tipped cane in the other. He was perhaps five foot nine, and his thick lenses only magnified the fact that his eyes were hopelessly clouded with cataracts. The right eye was pure milky white; the left navigated a curious circle every so often—down, to the left, and then up and behind the lid.

For a moment Katie just stared at the filthy, stained beige nylon shirt, the thin cotton pants held up by tattered suspenders that in turn kept slipping from his stooped shoulders. The tuning case looked disturbingly like a doctor's bag, and she remembered the Christmas when she was eight, when she had been too ill to leave the house and would wake from fevered nightmares to see the big black satchel at her bedside.

The piano tuner's fingers beat a silent tattoo on the handle of his cane.

"You must be Mr. Trister," Katie finally stammered. "Please come in. . . . I . . . I'm so glad you're here."

The old man grunted and tapped his way up the porch and through the door.

"You have a lovely house, Miss Prescott," he said in that same hushed tone, as if a baby slept nearby.

"Why, thank you," Katie replied, thinking that he couldn't possibly be seeing a thing, but she continued, "This used to be the music room years ago, when the original owners lived here."

"Isn't that fitting," Trister said and smiled. "It's almost like coming home again, isn't it?" He reached out and patted the Luchenbach.

Katie shivered involuntarily and excused herself as the piano man groped in his kit for his tools. Trister made her uncomfortable. She wasn't sure whether he was talking to her, to the piano, or to himself, for that matter. She began to rewire the doorbell and found her fingers unusually clumsy and uncooperative. As Trister tuned the strings one by one, she could hear him humming a song she hadn't thought of since she was a child—"Mairzy

Doats." How can he concentrate like that? she thought with irritation as she pushed the last wire into place.

"Miss Prescott?" Trister called. "Could I trouble you for a glass of water?"

Katie returned from the kitchen and set the glass on a coaster to the left of the keyboard. His hand met the glass as if directed by habit and returned it unerringly to its place.

"It's a lovely old piano, isn't it?" Trister said as he continued to chock the strings with his wedge-shaped strips of rubber.

"I fell in love with it the minute I saw it," Katie replied. "I don't know what it was about this one. . . . It . . . well, it seemed to be *meant* for me."

"Good, good." Trister nodded his head and smiled, then took another delicate sip from his water glass. The McDonaldland characters grinned up at his milky-white eyes . . . down, to the left, up and behind the lid . . . down, to the left, up and behind the lid . . .

"These Luchenbachs are very special, you know," he said. "Weren't many made quite like this one."

Katie couldn't help staring at his hand as he caressed the keys slowly, lovingly.

"You *know* this piano?" she finally asked.

"Oh yes, this little sweetie and I go way back . . . back to when my wife was pretty and my eyes were good." He chuckled and absently checked the clasps of his suspenders. "She was a real looker, Agnes was. Not so hot today, though, but then again, neither am I." He laughed outright. "No, I'm the piano man—or what's left of him," he said with a snaggle-toothed grin that Katie found no humor in at all.

"Have you always lived alone?" he asked abruptly.

"Yes," Katie replied before she realized it. "I mean, *no*," she said quickly, and a little too loudly.

"We all live alone in a way, Miss Prescott," Trister said softly.

Katie sat silently, angry with herself and the flush of heat on her cheeks.

"Gifted people very often choose to live alone," he continued. "You have a gift too, Miss Prescott, a talent."

"No, I don't," Katie said, but the words sounded far away.

Trister nodded his head and smiled, and Katie thought she heard him say, "Good, good," but was not sure. She felt small and cold and confused, and could not stop watching Trister's hands as he chocked and tuned, chocked and tuned.

"Oh, and Miss Prescott, you're missing a wire on the second B above middle C . . . right here." He reached out and played the note. "Can you tell the difference?"

He played an octave below and one above for Katie to compare. She was amazed at his complete command of the keyboard, his ability to find the right note without seeming to orient himself to the keyboard in any way. She remembered being drilled in theory by a teacher who demanded perfection and punished each incorrect note with a wooden ruler across the knuckles.

"When I replaced the keys I must not have noticed that wire." He gathered his tools and deftly replaced them in his case. "I'll call you next week and we'll set a date to fix it."

As he rose to leave, he knocked over his glass. It bounced, launching ice cubes across the living room floor. Katie knelt to retrieve the ice and to catch the rolling glass.

"Don't worry, it didn't break," she said.

"I know." Trister started for the door, but turned and looked down at Katie. Several moments went by as his left eye went down, to the left, and up behind the lid, over and over again. "Do you know what 'trister' means?" he asked.

The melting cubes were burning her palm with icy fire, and from her position on the floor, the piano man looked immense.

"It's from the Middle English word 'triste,' but it meant the same as tryst does today. A trister was the hunter who stayed hidden while the rest of the hunting party drove the game in his direction—he had a tryst to keep with his quarry, so to speak. Well, it most certainly was a pleasure. I'll be in touch." With that, he turned and tapped his way to the front door.

Katie remained kneeling for several minutes until she realized a number of things at once. Her hand was painfully cold, her knees ached, and she had left Mr. Trister on his own to make his way down the stairs to wait for his ride. She went to the front porch, but there was no one there. She didn't remember a door slamming or hearing a car pull away. The late-summer afternoon seemed unusually silent, and although the sky was a crisp, clear blue, the air felt threatening, as if a thunderstorm were about to break.

Pensively, Katie returned to the Luchenbach and cracked her knuckles to ease the constant tinge of arthritis in her left hand. She noticed that Mr. Trister had neglected to lower the top of the piano. Inside, written in pencil on the backboard, she saw names and dates:

KAUFMAN 6–4–79
ALLEN 8–6–78
SHUTTS 7–4–77
OTT 9–22–76
NELSEN 8–6–75

Katie stood on tiptoe and peered inside, but the list continued further than she could see. She wondered why Mr. Trister hadn't added his name and the date to that day's tuning, then she remembered that he couldn't *see* the list. *Damn* that creepy old man, she thought, as she lowered the lid and then thumbed through a stack of sheet music.

Katie turned to page one of Richard Rodgers's *Slaughter on Tenth Avenue* and struck the first chord. It sounded harsh and loud, like a handclap in a still, bare room. She stopped, frowned, moistened her lips with the tip of her tongue, and tried again. The striptease dance—allegretto. Fight between Junior and Misha—allegro. Junior dances with Vera's dead body—andante doloroso. Katie felt as if there was an invisible audience in the room, a thousand pairs of ears listening, appraising, judging. Once again it mattered. Once again her performance had to sound right, flow right, *be* right. Her back started to hurt; her hands ached, her eyes felt tired and gritty. The simplest sonata began to take enormous concentration. Her mistakes sounded louder now, more glaring, more frequent.

Soon, exhausted and angry, Katie tumbled onto the overstuffed blue and white sofa and slept fitfully, the beat of her pulse keeping time with a metronome that went down, to the left, and up, over and over again, while a voice whispered, "Good, good," so closely to her ear that she could feel its hot breath.

It was near midnight when she awoke, sprawled uncomfortably across the sofa, her mouth dry and cottony like the keyless piano in the store. Sofa cushions were strewn on the floor and she stumbled over them as she wobbled into the kitchen for a drink.

Sipping tepid orange juice by the light of the refrigerator bulb, Katie felt as if she'd polished off a bottle of cheap whiskey during one of her depression drunks. She squinted across the counter, but no empty bottle of Chymes Canadian Royal mocked her as it had so many times before. I have a gift, all right, she thought bitterly. A real talent. You were right about that, Mr. Trister. I have talent. All dressed up and nowhere to go.

The tiny refrigerator light hurt her eyes. She closed the door and leaned against it in the dark while she finished her juice.

Seated at the piano once again, Katie felt across the keys in the dark. She went over each uneven edge with her fingertips, trying to understand why she had bought the Luchenbach in the first place. She hadn't felt this way since she left home, this combination of the exhilarating power of musical ability and the paralyzing fear that she just wasn't good enough. Not good enough for Carnegie Hall, not good enough for her parents, not good enough for anyone. We may all live alone in a way, Mr. Trister, but some of us are just plain alone, Katie thought.

She began to play, but there was no grace to her music—no lilting quality to the tones. She felt as if she were merely pounding the keys with slender mallets of flesh, and that the Luchenbach, angered by such treatment, was becoming less and less responsive. The action felt stiffer, the hammers flailed aimlessly, the strings refused to resonate; each note was swallowed up by the thick, hot darkness. Incomplete passages of Chopin, Bartók, and Clementi teased her ears and her fingers tripped awkwardly across the keys like clumsy dancers.

Finally, in tears, Katie tried to play children's songs with one finger . . . "Chopsticks," "London Bridge," "Mary Had a Little Lamb" . . . but she found that she was unable to remember even a simple tune from start to finish. It was as if the music was trapped inside her head, unable to come out, unable to be remembered. After a long silence, the barest hint of a melody whispered in her ear—familiar, but she couldn't quite grasp it. She began to follow it, note by note . . .

G, E, down to middle C, A, G, A, back to middle C, E, G, E, A, E, G, E . . .

Her index fingers pecked out the proper notes, matching the melody in her head . . .

F, G, F, E, F, D, down to G below middle C, up an octave to G, E . . .

And while she played, head bent and eyes straining through the darkness at the back of her hands, another hand slid from beneath the hinged music desk and grasped her wrists in a cold, steely grip. Katie bolted backward, kicking at the piano and knocking the chair over, but the hand maintained its hold.

She tugged and lashed out in wild panic, grunting, panting, too afraid to cry out. The hand began to pull her toward the piano—slowly, so very slowly—and Katie fought to get away. She leaned forward, bit the hand, and gagged. It tasted of age and dust and death. And it was strong. Impossibly strong. It continued to pull her into the piano, inch by inch, oblivious to her struggle. Its cruel fingers pressed tightly into her flesh and the tuning pegs dug into her back as she was drawn into the cold labyrinth of wood and wire and metal teeth.

Then Katie heard something that made her stop struggling for an instant. A distinct humming. A *voice* humming. Finding her breath at last, she screamed for help, kicked, cried, and thrashed about inside the piano, becoming more entangled by the second. The wires cut into her arms like blades of ice and the little wooden hammers pummeled back at her agitated movements.

The humming grew steadily louder, and Katie suddenly stopped. It was coming from the thing that continued to draw her deeper into the piano . . . and when she recognized the tune—the same tune she had been trying to play, the same tune she had had to listen to over and over all afternoon—a sickening shiver raised each hair on end and tiny rivulets of cold sweat became itching, burning, unreachable rivers. In the darkness, two milky-white eyes opened and peered at her. One was stable; the other navigated a curious circle—down, to the left, and up. Katie felt a damp, callused hand begin to fondle her neck, so slowly, so tenderly. No matter how loudly she screamed, she could still hear "Mairzy Doats."

When it was silent at last, a gnarled fist grasping the worn stub of a number-two pencil poised at the top of the list of names inside the piano and, perfectly in line with the others and in the same, peculiar spidery handwriting, wrote:

PRESCOTT   8–30–80

Introduction

An editor does not dare pass up a story like this.

FOLLOWING THE WAY

by Alan Ryan

Twenty years ago, in my senior year at Regis High School—a very fine and very private Jesuit preparatory school on the upper east side of Manhattan—vocations to the priesthood were the order of the day. As I recall, twenty-five or so of the one hundred and fifty members of my graduating class entered the seminary, most of them, not surprisingly, choosing the Society of Jesus. Not all of them are priests today. (For that matter, not all of the Jesuits who taught me at Regis are priests today.) But vocations were in the air in that school, then half a century old already, and I suspect that, even today, few boys pass through their four years of study without at least considering, however briefly, the possibility of the priesthood. I did. I think we all did. We had behind us, though immediate in our thoughts, a long and impressive tradition. And before us we had some very powerful male role models: priests whom we respected as teachers and scholars, men who had devoted their lives to God, to an ideal, and to us, men who were clearly happy in their work, and who were, at the same time, interesting. The exceptions—sadly and most notably, the headmaster of the school during my four years there—only emphasized the union of humanity and spirituality in the others. For a boy with the inclination, the lure was hard to resist.

Those boys who were so inclined naturally sought and found willing advisers among the priests and scholastics on the faculty. But the rest of us—a spiritually silent majority—were not overlooked by the ever-thorough Jesuits—oh, no—and, sometime during the first half of our senior year, each of us was invited into the

office of the Jesuit student counselor for a private chat. (I should
stress that there was no coercion here. At Regis we were seldom
"ordered" to do things; rather, we were "invited.") I remember
that, in my case, the priest—a kind, charming, very learned, and
often sickly man named William Day—who will figure prominently
in this chronicle of my vocation—engaged me in polite conversation for some minutes without raising the question that I knew
very well was at hand. The idea was that, if I had been reluctant
to acknowledge interest in the priesthood before now, this would
be my golden opportunity. I said nothing, and the poor man—as
he had no doubt done a hundred times in the previous two weeks
—had to broach the subject himself. Had I, he wondered casually,
ever considered becoming a priest? Yes, Father, I answered, I
had. Ah ha, he said, nodding gently. You've thought about it? Oh,
yes, I said. And what conclusion have you reached? It's not for
me, I said. Oh, he said, I see, and stopped nodding. And why is
that? he asked. Sex, I said. Apparently I said it with such convic-
tion that he was thoroughly convinced of my thinking on the subject and ended the conversation there and then.

But times and people change.

I went from four years with the Jesuits at Regis High School to
four years with the Jesuits at Fordham University. The Lincoln
Center campus was then only in the planning stage, and I was always glad I missed it. (Leave it to the Jebbies, we joked in the
cafeteria, to luck into expensive real estate and a good address.)
Like my classmates who accompanied me from Regis, I was
happy to exchange East 84th Street for the Rose Hill campus in
the north Bronx. The Third Avenue El still rattled past the campus then and the traffic was heavy and noisy on Fordham Road
and Webster Avenue, but the campus itself was an island, a green
and peaceful island apart from the world outside, firmly anchored
in bedrock by the pylons of handsome Keating Hall, its gray field-
stone blocks and clock tower so quintessentially representative of
American college architecture that fashion photographers and TV
crews filming commercials were often to be found on its steps. It
was a lovely place: the green expanse of Edwards Parade, the
rose-covered trellis in the square beside Dealy Hall, the musty an-

tique air of Collins Theatre, the richly detailed chapel that sang aloud to God, all of it peaceful and lovely.

The Jesuit priests there were much the same as those at Regis—a little more worldly, perhaps, a little wittier, a little more acerbic, a little more eccentric, but, in all that mattered, essentially the same. I admired them, admired the wit and the learning and the grace with which they moved through the world, the casual self-assurance, the *flair*. My father had died when I was a child and there were no other male relatives close by, so, lacking a model at home, and primed by four years at Regis, I naturally turned toward these men and sought to emulate them. It was not a bad choice.

I spent most of my time in college—intellectually, at least, and psychologically, I suppose—as a young gentleman in a nineteenth-century novel might have spent his time at Oxford. I wrote some poetry, submitted some stories to *The New Yorker* and the *Atlantic Monthly*, and spent a great deal of time pursuing women. I read—in Greek—Plato and Aristotle and Euripides and, to lighten the mood, Sappho and the poets. (Xenophon and Homer had been amply translated at Regis.) Horace, Catullus, and Livy held sway in Latin class. Ronsard, Racine, Flaubert, Camus, Ionesco, were read in French; Dante in Italian; Chaucer in Middle English. I majored in French for three of the four years, studied linguistics and the gothic novel and early American literature and European history and "gentlemen's biology" and did some Russian on the side, in addition to the equivalent of full majors in philosophy and theology that were required of all undergraduates at the time. Most of my teachers were Jesuit priests.

One afternoon in the spring of my junior year, I was coming down the steps of Keating Hall when I met that same Jesuit who had offered me my golden opportunity to confess a vocation at Regis. I had heard through the Jesuit grapevine that he'd been unwell and was now at Fordham, taking courses and regaining his strength. It was a warm day—not warm by summer standards, but warm for April after winter's chill—but the priest was buttoned up tight in a black raincoat that obviously still had its winter lining in place. I knew him to be in his early forties, but a casual observer might have guessed him ten years older than that. Looks can be deceiving.

"Hello, Father Day."

He slowed his already slow progress up the shallow steps of Keating and mumbled the half-smiled greeting teachers offer former students whom they no longer recall. But I had stopped where I was and apparently something compelled him to raise his eyes to my face, and when he did so, he halted too. Eyes momentarily alive, he scrutinized my face.

"Regis," he said.

I smiled and said yes.

"Three years ago?"

"Yes."

"Of course," he said. His eyes narrowed, and before I could remind him myself, he told me my name, as casually as if I'd last been with him yesterday.

These Jesuits, I thought.

I was about to ask him how he was, but he spoke before I could.

"Sex," he said, and we laughed together, remembering. "Most succinct answer I ever had," he said, "and a good one, a good one."

We stood on the steps, chatting easily and pleasantly. He seemed eager to know how I was doing at Fordham, what I was studying, who my teachers were, what plans I had for the future. In high school there had been much talk about "the Regis spirit," one manifestation of which was the invisible but substantial tie that links alumni whenever they encounter each other in the world in later years. It can make confidants of strangers, this common baggage of shared learning, assumptions, attitudes. Father Day, I knew, was a Regis man himself, and I was warmed by this tangible evidence of the Regis spirit in action. After a few minutes, he suggested that we go to the Campus Center for coffee—his treat—and since I had been heading there myself when we met, I readily agreed.

We sat for two hours, happily telling stories about mutual acquaintances at Regis, stories that often made us laugh as we compared quite different versions of the same events as seen from the sides of students and faculty. Then the conversation gradually drifted back to me and my life at Fordham and my future and I wasn't even surprised when Father Day inquired casually if I had ever thought again about the possibility of a priestly vocation. I had, of course. In a setting like that—spiritual, intellectual, psychological—one does. It was—and here I measure my words with extra caution—a not unattractive possibility. But, still, it was not attractive enough to win me over. My interest in that direction was based primarily on practical and pragmatic considerations, and definitely not on any "call from God to His service" that I had felt. He smiled understandingly when I told him I had thought about it but my conclusion remained the same.

"No harm in asking," he said, and maintained his slight smile. I agreed.

"And no harm in thinking about it further," he said, the smile unchanged.

I agreed again.

"Will you?" he asked.

"Think about it further?"

"Yes."

"All right," I said, my smile matching his. "Couldn't hurt."

"Right," he said. "Couldn't hurt. Which is the punch line of an old vaudeville joke." He leaned back in his chair. "Ten minutes before he's going on stage, see, this famous comedian dies in his dressing room and the stage manager has to . . ."

We talked another twenty minutes or so before I had to leave for a late class. Even then, as I rose and gathered my books, it did not occur to me that Father Day, when we first met on the steps of Keating Hall, had been heading into the building and had changed his direction entirely to spend two and a half hours talking with me in the cafeteria.

When we parted at the front doors of the Campus Center, we assured each other how good it had been to talk and sincerely wished each other well. We both felt it, I was certain: the Regis spirit, made flesh.

It was three years later and I was twenty-four, a graduate student at UCLA, before I saw him again. Either because I had promised or because it was inevitable, I had indeed been thinking further about the priesthood.

Los Angeles, UCLA, Westwood Village, and Santa Monica (where I had a furnished apartment just off Wilshire Boulevard, about ten blocks from the beach), seem unlikely places to be thinking about withdrawing—to a degree, at least—from the world and devoting one's life to the service of God. I did, however, and although I was aware of the contrast between my own thinking and that of those around me, I continued to consider, if only in a pragmatic way, the possibility of becoming a priest.

The idea had much to recommend it. I was alone in the world now, my mother having died in an automobile accident in Switzerland during the summer following my graduation from Fordham. I went to California an orphan, lacking even brothers, sisters, aunts, uncles, cousins, to form a family. There was, in that regard, no one to take into account but myself. On the other hand, a religious community could readily fill the need for a structure and a sense of purpose and continuity in my life.

Furthermore, my mother's death had left me financially independent as well, thanks to her firm belief in large amounts of travel insurance, and my independence and self-sufficiency made me, I think it fair to say, rather more mature in my judgments than others in their early twenties, and rather more than I might have been myself in different circumstances.

As for the "sex" I had mentioned to Father Day half a dozen years earlier as an overriding factor in my negative decision, it had proved, as I grew older, less of a problem. To speak the truth, I was no virgin, and I think my needs and appetites at the time, during those years, were as normal as anyone else's, which may prove a mystery to laymen who think that priests and future priests are sometimes spared the hunger. They are not; I can vouch for it. But I did find, through necessity of time and circumstance, that the urge can be controlled, not through any secret vice, which is most often only a form of self-torture, serving merely to remind us of what we lack, but through a careful discipline of the will.

In a practical sense, my life was right for the priesthood. In a psychological sense—and a practical one—I was comfortable with the idea; I would teach in any case. In a spiritual sense, it meant nothing at all; I felt no infusion of God's spirit, no call to His service, and began truly to wonder if that last were really needed.

And then, once again, I ran into Father Day.

It was early May, the end of the academic year, the oral exams for my master's degree successfully completed, and nothing before me but a summer of travel. I had driven back to the campus to return some books and was sitting near the entrance to Royce Hall, enjoying the California sun, reading a newspaper, and listening to the noon carillon concert from the undergraduate library. I had nothing to do for the afternoon, nothing to do, in fact, for a week until my plane left for Europe.

I heard a voice speak my name and say, "Well, hello."

I raised my head and there was Father Day.

He looked much the same as he had three years before. In fact, we might almost have been back on the steps of Keating Hall at Fordham, amid the elms and the dogwood, rather than here beside the Spanish architecture of Royce Hall, amid the bird of paradise plants and the palms. He still looked older than his years—the same observation I had made at Fordham, the last time I'd seen him. And he was still somewhat overdressed. The sun was warm, with only a gentle breeze blowing across the campus, but Father Day wore black woolen slacks and a black turtleneck shirt under a battered gray tweed sport jacket. Even discarding the standard clerical garb, as Jesuits feel so free to do, he had not indulged in any great license. He looked, as he had before, like a man recovering from a long illness, which indeed he was. Thin blood, I thought, meant to thicken in the sun. I said it was good to see him and that he was looking well.

We satisfied each other's curiosity and quickly provided basic information. He told me he had been on campus the whole spring term. Nominally, he was here to take courses in comparative religion. Actually, he was in California for a rest to build up his strength. He spent part of his time helping out with light duties—mass and confession—in a parish church in North Hollywood, where he was living now. He was thinking of accepting a teaching position he'd been offered at Loyola University. I told him that, unless a decent teaching position came along for me, I planned to start work on my doctorate in the fall term and, in that case, would no doubt turn into the archetypal perennial student. He smiled a little ruefully and said that it wasn't such a bad life, and then we were laughing together.

And before I realized it, we were once again talking about me and I was, once again, admitting that thoughts of the priesthood were still in my mind. And, again before I realized it, we had strolled from the campus out to Westwood Village and had found a quiet booth in a bar near the Bruin Theatre.

"You keep turning up in my life," I said when we had beers in front of us.

"Twice," he said.

"Twice is almost a pattern."

"Almost," he agreed.

"Maybe you're haunting me."

"Maybe," he said and took a long drink from his glass. "Or maybe God is haunting you through me."

I thought of all the practical reasons I had for taking Holy Orders, and of all the spiritual reasons I lacked. "Not bloody likely," I said.

"Oh?" It's a Jesuit habit to say that; it offers nothing but elicits much.

So I told him, told him all the wide range of my thoughts on the subject, told him how, although I had not reached a definitive conclusion, the inevitable answer, born of inertia, seemed certainly negative. He listened patiently, his face without expression, until I finished.

"So, then, you feel no call to the priesthood, no compulsion. Is that right?"

I shook my head. "None."

"The call can come in any variety of ways," he said. "The path to God is not a straight one."

"And there are many doors in the castle, yes, I know, Father."

"Don't be impatient."

"Sorry."

"Maybe I'm your call."

I looked at him then and, for a long moment, and for the first time, seriously wondered if perhaps he was right, perhaps he was truly haunting me.

"The path to God is not a straight one," I said, and we both smiled and relaxed, the moment of tension gone.

"If we run into each other like this again," he said, "it will definitely be a pattern."

"Indeed," I said.

"Patterns like that must be considered."

"All right," I said, "if we run into each other like this again, I'll grant you it constitutes a pattern."

"And you'll consider it?"

"The pattern?"

"The priesthood."

"Ah," I said. And a moment later: "All right."

"Good," he said. "I think this calls for another beer."

It was not three years this time, but six weeks, before I saw him again.

I took a place in the queue for tickets to the Royal Ballet at Covent Garden and there he was just in front of me. Neither of us realized it until he'd bought his ticket and turned away from the counter. Suddenly there we were. I quickly purchased my own ticket and followed him outside into Floral Street. A minute later, we were established in the Nag's Head a few doors away, two steins of cold lager before us.

"You're following me," I said. "It's beginning to look slightly sinister."

"Is it?" Jesuits love to ask questions.

"A bit. What are you doing here? I thought you were in Los Angeles."

"I was. Actually, in a way, I still am. I took the faculty position at Loyola and then rather lucked into a university travel grant. It was none of my doing, actually."

"I'll bet," I said lightly.

"Actually," he replied.

He looked, it hardly seems necessary to mention, quite the same as before. The weather in London was cool and damp even in summer, but he was still overdressed. It seemed a permanent fea-

ture of his appearance. Apparently the California sun had not suc-
ceeded in thickening his blood. I didn't imagine the chilly air of
London would accomplish much in that line, but the thought
seemed not to have occurred to him.

"Did you follow me here?"

He shook his head, a gentle smile on his lips. "Impossible," he
said.

That, of course, was the truth, and I knew it already. Apart
from the obvious reasons, if he'd appeared just behind me in the
queue, I might have doubted, but he had been there in front of me
when I arrived, no question about it, and I did not.

"Then you're haunting me," I said.

"So it appears," he replied. He lifted his glass and in one long
drink finished off the beer. "I have to be on my way," he said.
"Let's meet for dinner."

We agreed on seven-thirty at Romano Santi in Soho, and a moment later he was gone. I stayed longer in the Nag's Head, ordered
another lager and drank it as slowly as the first. After that, I
walked over to Charing Cross Road and spent the rest of the afternoon in the National Portrait Gallery. I barely saw the faces in
the paintings. I could see only the face of Father Day, haunting
me wherever I went.

During the meal, we limited the conversation to general topics.
Afterward, he invited me back to his house for drinks. As we rode
in the taxi the length of Oxford Street from Soho to Notting Hill
Gate, and then pulled up in front of a lovely home in Kensington
Park Road which he was renting for the summer, I wondered what
sort of travel grant provided that sort of living allowance. These
Jesuits, I thought. They're like some fine old family, ripe with old
money.

"Shall we sit in the sitting room?" he said as he gestured me inside. "It seems only proper."

By that point, I was half expecting servants, but the house was
empty. We'd had chianti with the meal and he suggested a lighter
burgundy now. He poured the wine himself. When we were settled
in easy chairs, he wasted no time.

"I think you have a vocation," he said. "Perhaps you feel no call, nothing of the sort you've thought all along you ought to feel, but a vocation nonetheless."

"Why?" I asked. I tried to sip my drink calmly.

"Why do you have a vocation or why do I say that?"

"Both." These Jesuits, I thought again. They never stop. It comes with long practice.

"Both," he repeated, in a tone that reminded me of the classroom. "As for the first, why you have a vocation, I couldn't begin to tell you. I almost hate to say it because it sounds entirely too pat, but it's not for us to question the ways of God."

"Just lucky, I guess." I said it as much to provoke him as for anything else.

"I guess," he said, and studied me curiously, as if wondering at the oddness of God's dealings among men. While he studied me, I had the opportunity to do the same with him, and realized that, at least for the moment, he no longer looked as sickly as he had before. He looked, rather, like a man with a definite job to do, a man with a clear purpose.

"As for the second point," he said, "why I'm telling you this, remember that Christ taught us to be fishers of men."

"The wise fisherman doesn't cast his net at random," I said.

"Nicely put."

"Why me, Father?"

"You're the type."

"*What* type?"

"Why, the priestly type, of course."

"That's a tautology."

"You'll make a splendid Jesuit," he laughed. "Here, let me top up your glass."

We sat together in silence for a while, with only the wine and our thoughts.

"Have you not noticed," he said at last, "that I seem to keep recurring in your life? Oh, never mind, of course you have." He leaned forward in his chair. "Answer a question. The Church will last forever, will it not? Until, would it be safe to say, the end of time, at least? Agreed?"

I nodded.

"Why?" he snapped. "How can that be?"

I hesitated, answers that had once seemed so clear—or at least so thoroughly assumed—now failing me.

"I've forgotten a lot of my catechism," I said to cover my hesitation.

"You haven't forgotten *this* catechism," he said. "These are answers you never knew. What is the central fact in your belief?"

"That Christ was the Son of God."

"And?"

"That He died on the cross. The sacrifice of the cross."

"The sacrifice of the cross," he repeated. "And what is the central practice, the central event, of your worship?"

"The Eucharist," I said. "The sacrifice of the mass."

"The sacrifice of the mass. Can you live forever?"

"Yes."

"How?"

"My soul is eternal. Listen, I—"

"You can live forever," he said.

I looked at him.

He said it again, more slowly. "You can live forever."

It was my turn. "How?" I said.

He raised his wine glass toward me. It reflected the light from a lamp and glowed ruby red.

"This is the cup of my blood," he said. "Take and drink of it." He was smiling.

I looked from his face to the glass of wine, held aloft as it might be held above the altar, offered to God and displayed to the faithful, with the words of consecration transforming it to blood.

Of course. At last. Here was the epiphany I'd sought, the obvious thing, long regarded but never seen till now: the realization, revelation, moment, insight, the ancient sacred secret of the Church. I was surprised only in that I felt no surprise.

I thought of all the priests I'd known, thought of all the times I'd been at mass and heard a priest murmur those words, transforming wine into the blood of Jesus Christ. Thought of the cross. Thought of the ages the Church, alone of all institutions, had lasted already. Thought of the ages ahead. And, again very practical, thought of myself standing before an altar, speaking those very same words, ordained with the power of transforming ordinary wine into sacred blood, an endless supply for an endless life-time. I held my breath a moment, then looked back at Father Day.

"Do the others know?" I asked. "Or is it only the Jesuits?"

When he was done laughing, he caught his breath and said, "Oh, this is definitely not a perfect world. Yes, the others know." And he was off again into gales of laughter.

When he'd caught his breath a second time, he raised his glass in a silent toast. Then he set it down, rose from his chair, and came and stood beside me. He bent forward and gently—very gently—placed his lips against my neck.

This was all some years ago.

What follows is forever.

I am a priest and shall remain so. I rest eternal in the bosom of the Lord. I am following the way. I am satisfied.

Introduction

It happens—a writer creates a character that of its own volition spills over from one story to another, one novel to another. But when the writer is as astute and talented as Chelsea Quinn Yarbro, she knows when the themes have been explored as much as they should, when anything more might too easily be labeled excess. This, then, is the last story in the cycle of le Comte de Saint-Germain.

RENEWAL

by Chelsea Quinn Yarbro

With bloodied hands, James pulled the ornate iron gates open and staggered onto the long drive that led to the château. Although he was dazed, he made sure the gates were properly shut before starting up the tree-lined road. How long ago he had made his first journey here—and how it drew him now. He stared ahead, willing the ancient building to appear out of the night as he kept up his dogged progress toward the one place that might provide him the shelter he so desperately needed.

When at last the stone walls came into view, James was puzzled to hear the sound of a violin, played expertly but fragmentally, as if the music were wholly personal. James stopped and listened, his cognac-colored eyes warming for the first time in three days. Until that moment, the only sound he had remembered was the grind and pound of guns. His bleary thoughts sharpened minimally and he reached up to push his hair from his brow. Vaguely he wondered who was playing—and why—for Montalia had an oddly deserted look to it: the grounds were overgrown and only two of the windows showed lights. This was more than wartime precaution, James realized, and shambled toward the side door he had used so many times in the past, the first twinges of real fear giving him a chill that the weather had not been able to exert.

The stables smelled more of motor oil than horses, but James recognized the shape of the building, and limped into its shadow with relief. Two lights, he realized, might mean nothing more than most of the servants had retired for the night, or that shortages of fuel and other supplies forced the household to stringent economies. He leaned against the wall of the stable and gathered his courage to try the door. At least, he told himself, it did not appear that the château was full of Germans. He waited until the violin was pouring out long cascades of sound before he reached for the latch, praying that if the hinges squeaked, the music would cover it.

In the small sitting room, Saint-Germain heard the distant whine of an opening door and his bow hesitated on the strings. He listened, his expanded senses acute, then sat back and continued the *Capriccio* he had been playing, letting the sound guide the solitary intruder. He gave a small part of his attention to the unsteady footfalls in the corridor, but for the most part, he concentrated on the long pattern of descending thirds of the cadenza. Some few minutes later, when he had begun one of the Beethoven romanzas, a ragged figure clutching a kitchen knife appeared in the doorway and emerged uncertainly from the darkness into the warmth of the hearthlight and the single kerosene lantern. Saint-Germain lowered his violin and gave the newcomer an appraising stare. His dark eyes narrowed briefly, then his brows raised a fraction as he recognized the man. "You will not need that knife, Mister Tree."

He had expected many things, but not this lone, elegant man. James shook his head, his expression becoming more dazed than ever. "I . . ." He brought a grimy, bruised hand to his eyes and made a shaky attempt at laughter which did not come off. He coughed once, to clear his voice. "When I got here and heard music . . . I thought that . . . I don't know what." As he spoke he reached out to steady himself against the back of one of the three overstuffed chairs in the fine stone room, which was chilly in spite of the fire. "Excuse me. . . . I'm not . . . myself."

"Yes, I can see that," Saint-Germain said with gentleness, knowing more surely than James how unlike himself he was. He stood to put his violin into its velvet-lined case, then tucked the loosened bow into its holder before closing the top. This done, he set the case on the occasional table beside his chair and turned to James. "Sit down, Mister Tree. Please." It was definitely a command, but one so kindly given that the other man complied at once, dropping gratefully into the chair which had been supporting him. The knife clattered to the floor, but neither paid any attention to it.

"It's been . . . a while," James said distantly, looking up at the painting over the fireplace. Then his gaze fell on Saint-Germain and he saw the man properly for the first time.

Le Comte was casually dressed by his own exacting standards: a black hacking jacket, a white shirt and black sweater under it, and black trousers. There were black ankle-high jodhpur boots on his small feet, the heels and soles unusually thick. Aside from a silver signet ring, he wore no jewelry. "Since you have been here? More than a decade, I would suppose."

"Yes." James shifted in the chair, his movements those of utter exhaustion. "This place . . . I don't know why." Only now that he had actually arrived at his goal did he wonder what had driven him to seek it out. Indistinct images filtered through his mind, most of them senseless, one or two of them frightening.

"On Madelaine's behalf, I'm pleased to welcome you back. I hope you will stay as long as you wish to." He said this sincerely, and watched James for his response.

"Thanks. I don't know what . . . thanks." In this light and with the abuses of the last few days, it was not possible to see how much the last ten years had favored James Emmerson Tree. His hair had turned from glossy chestnut to silver without loss of abundance; the lines of his face had deepened but had not become lost in fretwork or pouches, so that his character was cleanly incised, delineated in strong, sharp lines. Now, with smudges of dirt and dried blood on him, it was not apparent that while at thirty he had been good-looking, at fifty he was superbly handsome. He fingered the tear on his collar where his Press tag had been. "I thought . . . Madelaine might have been . . ."

"Been here?" Saint-Germain suggested as he drew one of the other chairs closer to where James sat. "I am sorry, Mister Tree. Madelaine is currently in South America."

"Another expedition?" James asked, more forlorn than he knew.

"Of course. It's more circumspect to stay there than to go to Greece or Africa just now—or wouldn't you agree?" He spoke slowly, deliberately and in English for the first time. "I would rather be assured of her safety than her nearness, Mister Tree."

James nodded absently, then seemed at last to understand what Saint-Germain had said, for he looked up sharply and said in a different voice, "God, yes. Oh God, yes."

"I had a letter from her not long ago. Perhaps you would care to read it later this evening?" He did not, in fact, want to share the contents of Madelaine's letter with James; it was too privately loving for any eyes but his, yet he knew that this man loved her with an intensity that was only exceeded by his own.

"No," James said after a brief hesitation. "So long as she's okay, that's all that matters. If anything happened to her, after this, I think I'd walk into the path of a German tank." His mouth turned up at the corners, quivered, and fell again into the harsh downward curve that had become characteristic in the last month. He looked down at his ruined jacket and plucked at one of the frayed tears.

Saint-Germain watched this closely, then asked, "Has the fighting been very bad?"

"What's very bad? Some days we kill more than they do, and some days they kill more. It sickens me." He turned toward the fire and for a little time said nothing; Saint-Germain respected his silence. Finally James sighed. "Is there anyone else here at Montalia?"

"My manservant Roger, but no one other than he." Again Saint-Germain waited, then inquired, "Is there something you require, Mister Tree? I would recommend a bath and rest to begin with."

This time James faltered noticeably. "It's funny; I really don't know what I want." He gave Saint-Germain a quick, baffled look. "I wanted to be here. But now that I am, I'm too tired to care."

His eyes met Saint-Germain's once, then fell away. "It doesn't make much sense."

"It makes admirable sense," Saint-Germain told him, shaking his head as he studied James.

"I'm probably hungry and sore, too, but, I don't know . . ." He leaned back in the chair, and after a few minutes while Saint-Germain built up the fire, he began to talk in a quiet, remote ramble. "I went home in '31; Madelaine might have mentioned it."

"Yes," Saint-Germain said as he poked at the pine log; it crackled and its sap ran and popped on the dry bark.

"It was supposed to be earlier, but what with the Crash, they weren't in any hurry to bring one more hungry reporter back to St. Louis. So Crandell—he was my boss then—extended my assignment and, when he died, Sonderson—who replaced him—gave me another eighteen months before asking me to come back. It was strange, being back in the States after more than thirteen years in Europe. You think you know how you'll feel, but you don't. You think it will be familiar and cozy, but it isn't. I felt damn-all odd, I can tell you. People on the street looked so . . . out of place. Of course, the Depression was wrecking everything in the cities, but it was not only that. What worried me was hearing the same old platitudes everyone had been using in 1916. I couldn't believe it. With everything that had happened, there was no comprehension that the world had changed. It was so different, in a way that was so complete that there was nothing the change did not touch. People kept about getting back to the old ways without understanding that they could not do that ever again . . ."

"There never is," Saint-Germain interjected softly. He was seated once again in the high-backed overstuffed chair.

". . . no matter what." James broke off. "Maybe you're right," he concluded lamely and stared at the fire. "I've been cold."

"In time you will be warm again, Mister Tree," Saint-Germain said and rose to pick up a silver bell lying on the table beside his violin case. "Would you like to lie down? You could use rest, Mister Tree." His manner was impeccably polite, but James sensed that he would do well to cooperate with the suggestion.

"Sure," was James's quiet response. "Sure, why not."

"Excellent, Mister Tree." He rang the bell, and within two minutes, a sandy-haired man of middle height, middle build, and middle age came into the room. "Roger, this is Madelaine's great good friend, James Emmerson Tree. He has gone through an . . . ordeal." One of Saint-Germain's brows rose sharply and Roger recognized it for the signal it was.

"How difficult for him," Roger said in a neutral voice. "Mister Tree, if you will let me attend to you . . ."

James shook his head. "I can manage for myself," he said, not at all sure that he could.

"Nonetheless, you will permit Roger to assist you. And when you have somewhat recovered, we will attend to the rest of it."

"The rest of it?" James echoed as he got out of the chair, feeling horribly grateful for Roger's proffered arm.

"Yes, Mister Tree, the rest of it." He smiled his encouragement, but there was little amusement in his countenance.

"Yeah, I guess," James responded vaguely and allowed himself to be guided into the dark hallway.

The bathroom was as he remembered it—large, white-tiled, and old-fashioned. The tub stood on gilt crocodile feet and featured elaborate fixtures of the sort that had been in vogue eighty years before. James regarded it affectionately while Roger helped to take off his damaged clothing. "I've always liked that tub," he said when he was almost naked.

"It *is* something of a museum piece," Roger said, and James was free to assume he agreed.

The water billowed out of the taps steaming, but James looked at it with an unexpected disquiet. He was filthy, his muscles were stiff and sore, and there were other hurts on his body which he thought would welcome the water, but at the last moment he hesitated, suppressing a kind of vertigo. With care, he steadied himself with one hand and said to Roger, who was leaving the room, "I'm worn out, that's what it is."

"Very likely," the manservant said in a neutral tone before closing the door.

As he stretched out in the tub, the anticipated relaxation did not quite happen. James felt his stiff back relax, but not to the point of letting him doze. He dismissed this as part of the aches and hurts that racked him. When he had washed away the worst of the grime, he looked over the damage he had sustained when he was thrown from the jeep. There was a deep weal down the inside of his arm. "Christ!" James muttered when he saw it, thinking he must have bled more than he had thought. Another deep cut on his thigh was red—but healing—and other lacerations showed no sign of infection. "Which is lucky," James remarked to the ceiling, knowing that he could never have come the long miles to Montalia if he had been more badly hurt. The other two reporters had not been so fortunate: one had been shot in the crossfire that wrecked the jeep and the other had been crushed as the jeep overturned.

This was the first time James had been able to remember the incident clearly—and it chilled him. How easy it would have been to have died with them. One different random factor and he would have been the one who was shot or crushed. With an oath, he got out of the tub and stood, shaking, on the cold tiles as the water drained away.

"I have brought you a robe," Roger said a few minutes later as he returned. "Your other garments are not much use any longer. I believe that there is a change of clothes in the armoire of the room you used to occupy."

"Hope I can still get into them," James said lightly in an attempt to control the fright that had gotten hold of him.

"You will discover that later, Mister Tree." He helped the American into the bathrobe he held, saying in a steady manner, "It's very late, Mister Tree. The sun will be up soon, in fact. Why don't you rest for now, and my master will see you when you have risen."

"Sounds good," James answered as he tied the sash. He wanted to sleep more than he could admit, more than he ever remembered wanting to. "I . . . I'll probably not get up until, oh, five or six o'clock."

"No matter, Mister Tree," Roger said and went to hold the door for James.

James woke from fidgety sleep not long after sunset. He looked blankly around the room Madelaine had given him so many years before and, for several minutes, could not recall how he had got there, or where he was. Slowly, as if emerging from a drugged stupor, he brought back the events of the previous night. There at the foot of the bed was the robe, its soft heavy wool familiar to his touch. Memories returned in a torrent as he sat up in bed: how many times he had held Madelaine beside him through the night and loved her with all his body and all his soul. He felt her absence keenly. At that, he remembered that Saint-Germain was at Montalia, and for the first time, James felt awkward about it. It was not simply that he was jealous, although that was a factor, but that he had never properly understood the man's importance in Madelaine's life.

He got out of bed and began to pace restlessly, feeling very hungry now, but oddly repulsed at the thought of food. "Rations," he said to the walls in a half-joking tone. "That's what's done it." Telling himself that he was becoming morbid, he threw off the robe, letting it lie in a heap in the nearest chair, and dressed in the slightly old-fashioned suit he had left here before returning to America. The trousers, he noticed, were a little loose on him now, and he hitched them up uneasily. He had neither belt nor suspenders for it, and might have to ask for one or the other. The jacket hung on him, and he reflected that he had not gone in for much exercise in the last few years until he had come back to Europe four months ago. He looked in vain for a tie and recollected that he had disdained them for a time. He would have to find something else.

At last he found a rolltop pullover at the bottom of one of the drawers and he gratefully stripped off his jacket and shirt to put it on. It was of soft tan wool, with one or two small holes on the right sleeve where moths had reached it, and it felt lovely next to his skin. With shirt and jacket once more donned, James felt that he presented a good enough appearance to venture down into the main rooms of the château.

He found his way easily enough, although the halls were dark. His eyes adjusted readily to this, and he told himself that, after all the nights when he and Madelaine had sought each other in the dim rooms and corridors, he should be able to find his way blindfolded. For the first time in several days, he chuckled.

"Something amuses you, Mister Tree?" said Saint-Germain

from behind him, his tone lightly remote as he approached. "I heard you come down the stairs a few minutes ago. I'm pleased you're up. I thought you might be . . . hungry."

"I was. I am," James said, turning to face the other man. "But there's . . ." He could not continue and was not certain why.

"For whatever consolation it may be to you, I do sympathize, Mister Tree," le Comte said slowly, looking up at the tall American. "It may surprise you to learn that it will be a while before you become used to your . . . transition." As he said this, his dark eyes met James's uncompromisingly.

"Transition?" James repeated with a bewildered smile. "I don't understand."

"Don't you?" Le Comte de Saint-Germain gave James another steady look and said cautiously, "Mister Tree, are you aware of what has happened to you?"

James laughed uneasily. "I think I've been hurt. I *know* I have. There are cuts on my arms and legs—a couple pretty serious." He cleared his throat nervously. "There were three of us in the jeep and there was an ambush. No one bothered to find out if we were Press, but I don't blame them for that. I don't know which side did it, really." He shook himself self-consciously. "Someone must have walked over my grave."

"Very astute, Mister Tree," Saint-Germain said compassionately.

"I don't remember much more than that. It *does* sound lame, doesn't it? But I don't."

"You recall being injured." He motioned toward the tall, studded doors that led to the small sitting room where James had found him the night before. "That is a start."

James fell into step beside the smaller man and was mildly startled to find that he had to walk briskly to keep up with Saint-Germain. "Actually it's all muddled. I remember the crossfire, and the jeep turning over, and being tossed into the air, but the rest is all . . . jumbled. I must have passed out, and didn't come to until after dark. I can't tell you what made me come here. I guess when you're hurt, you look for a safe place, and I've been here before, so . . ." He heard Saint-Germain close the door behind them and stopped to look about the sitting room.

"It seems eminently reasonable, Mister Tree," Saint-Germain told him as he indicated the chair James had occupied before.

"Good," James responded uneasily.

Saint-Germain drew up his chair; the firelight played on his face, casting sudden shadows along his brow, the line of his straight aslant nose, the wry sad curve of his mouth. Though his expression remained attentive, his eyes now had a sad light in them. "Mister Tree, how badly were you hurt?"

James was more disquieted now than ever and he tugged at the cuffs of his jacket before he answered. "It must have been pretty bad. But I walked here and I figure it's more than forty, maybe fifty miles from . . . where it happened." He ran one large hand through his silver hair. "Those cuts, though. Jesus! And I felt so . . . detached. Bleeding does that when it's bad—or so the medics told me. But I got up . . ."

"Yes," Saint-Germain agreed. "You got up."

"And I made it here . . ." With a sudden shudder, which embarrassed him, he turned away.

Saint-Germain waited until James was more composed, then said, "Mister Tree, you've had a shock—a very great shock—and you are not yet recovered from it. It will take more than a few minutes and well-chosen words of explanation to make you realize precisely what has occurred and what it will require of you."

"That sounds ominous," James said, forcing himself to look at Saint-Germain again.

"Not ominous," Saint-Germain corrected him kindly. "Demanding, perhaps, but not ominous." He stretched out his legs and crossed his ankles. "Mister Tree, Madelaine led me to understand that you were told about her true nature. Is this true?" Privately he knew it was, for Madelaine had confided all her difficulties with James over the years and Saint-Germain was aware of the American's stubborn disbelief in what he had been told.

"A little. I heard about the aristocratic family and looked them up." His square chin went up a degree or two. "She made some pretty wild claims . . ."

Saint-Germain cut him short. "Did you bother to investigate her claims?"

"Yes," James admitted, sighing. "I had to. When she told me

. . . those things, I had to find out if she had been making it up out of whole cloth." He rubbed his hands together, his nervousness returning.

"And what did you discover?" Saint-Germain's inquiry was polite, almost disinterested, but there was something in his dark eyes that held James's attention as he answered.

"Well, there was a Madelaine de Montalia born here in the eighteenth century. That was true. And she did . . . die in Paris in 1744. She was only twenty and I read that she was considered pretty." He paused. "The way Madelaine is pretty, in fact."

"Does that surprise you?" Saint-Germain asked.

"Well, the same family . . ." James began weakly, then broke off. "The portrait looked just like her—and she kept saying it was her." These words were spoken quickly and in an undervoice, as if James feared to let them have too much importance.

"But you did not believe her," Saint-Germain prompted him when he could not go on. "Why was that?"

"Well, you should have *heard* what she said!" James burst out, rising from the chair and starting to pace in front of the fireplace. "She told me. . . . Look, I know that you were her lover once. She didn't kid me about that. And you might not know the kinds of things she said about herself . . ." He stopped and stared down at the fire, thinking that he was becoming more famished by the minute. If he could eat, then he would not have to speak. Unbidden, the memories of the long evenings with Madelaine returned with full force to his thoughts. He pictured her dining room with its tall, bright windows, Madelaine sitting across from him or at the corner, watching him with delighted eyes as he ate. She never took a meal with him and he had not been able to accept her explanation for this. As he tried to recall the taste of the sauce Claude had served with the fish, he nearly gagged.

"I know what she told you," Saint-Germain said calmly, as if from a distance. "She told you almost twenty years ago that she is a vampire. You did not accept this, although you continued to love her. She warned you what would happen when you died and you did not choose to believe her. Yet she told you the truth, Mister Tree."

James turned around so abruptly that for a moment he swayed

on his feet. "Oh sure! Fangs and capes and graveyards and all the rest of it. Madelaine isn't any of those things."

"Of course not."

"And," James continued rather breathlessly now that he was started, "she said that you were . . . and that you were the one who changed her!" He had expected some reaction to this announcement, but had not anticipated that it would be a nod and a stern smile. "She said . . ." he began again, as if to explain more to Saint-Germain.

"I'm aware of that. She had my permission, but that was merely a formality." He sat a bit straighter in his chair as the significance of his words began to penetrate James's indignation. "She and I are alike in that way, now. It is correct: I did bring about her change, as she brought about yours." His steady dark eyes were unfaltering as they held James's.

"Come on," James persisted, his voice growing higher with tension. "You can't want her to say that about you. You can't."

"Well, in a general way I prefer to keep that aspect of myself private; yes," Saint-Germain agreed urbanely, "but it is the truth, nonetheless."

James wanted to yell so that he would not have to listen to those sensible words, so that he could shut out the quiet, contained man who spoke so reasonably about such completely irrational things. "Don't joke," he growled, his jaw tightening.

"Mister Tree," Saint-Germain said—and something in the tone of his voice insisted that James hear him out. The American journalist reluctantly fell silent. "Mister Tree, self-deception is not a luxury that we can afford. I realize that you have been ill-prepared for . . . recent events, and so I have restrained my sense of urgency in the hope that you would ask the questions for yourself. But you have not—and it isn't wise or desirable for you to continue in this way. No," he went on, not permitting James to interrupt, "you must listen to me for the time being. When I have done, I will answer any questions you have as forthrightly as possible; until then, be good enough to remain attentive and resist your understandable inclination to argue."

James was oddly daunted by the air of command that had come over le Comte, but he had many years' experience in concealing any awe he might feel, and so he clasped his hands behind his back and took a few steps away from the fire as if to compensate for the strength he sensed in Saint-Germain. "Okay; okay. Go on."

Saint-Germain's smile was so swift that it might not have occurred at all—there was a lift at the corners of his mouth and his expression was once again somber. "Madelaine took you as her lover sometime around 1920, as I recall, and it was in 1925 that she tried to explain to you what would become of you after you died." He saw James flinch at the last few words, but did not soften them. "Like Madelaine, you would rise from death and walk again, vampiric. As long as your nervous system is intact, you will have a kind of life in you, one that exerts a few unusual demands. You have some experience of them already. You are hungry, are you not? And yet you cannot bring yourself to eat. The notion of food is repulsive. We're very . . . specific in our nourishment, Mister Tree, and you must become accustomed to the new requirements. . . ."

"You're as bad as she is," James muttered, looking once toward the door as if he wanted to bolt from the room. He wanted to convince himself that the other man was a dangerous lunatic or a charlatan enjoying himself at James's expense, but there was undoubted sincerity in Saint-Germain's manner and a pragmatic attitude that was terribly convincing.

"Oh, I am much worse than Madelaine, Mister Tree. It was I who made her a vampire, back in the autumn of 1743." He frowned as James turned swiftly, violently away. "Your change was assured possibly as early as 1922, but Madelaine was so fearful of your hatred that it took her over two years to gather her courage to explain the hazard to you. You see, she loves you and the thought of your detestation was agony for her. She could not leave you unprepared, however, and eventually revealed . . ."

"This is crazy," James insisted to the ceiling; he could not bring himself to look at Saint-Germain. "Crazy."

"Do you appreciate the depth of her love?" Saint-Germain went on as if he had not heard James's outburst. "Your protection was more important to her than your good opinion. She risked being loathed so that you would not have to face your change in ignorance." He folded his arms. "And you make a paltry thing of her gift by refusing to admit that the change has happened."

James threw up his hands and strode away from the fireplace toward the farthest corner of the room. "This doesn't make any sense. Not any of it. You're talking like a madman." He could hear the unsteadiness of his voice and, with an effort of will, lowered and calmed it. "I remember what she told me about being a vampire. I didn't believe it then; you're right. I don't believe it now. And you keep talking as if something has happened to me. True enough. My jeep was shot out from under me, I've lost a lot of blood, and I've been wandering without food for over three days. No wonder I feel so . . . peculiar."

Slowly Saint-Germain got out of the chair and crossed the room toward James. His compelling eyes never left James's face and the quiet command of his well-modulated voice was the more authoritative for its lack of emotion. "Mister Tree, stop deluding yourself. When that jeep turned over, when you were thrown through the air, you suffered fatal injuries. You lay on the ground and bled to death. But death is a disease to which we are, in part, immune. When the sun set, you woke into . . . Madelaine's life, if you will." He stopped less than two strides from James. "Whether you wish to believe it or not, you are a vampire, Mister Tree."

"Hey, no . . ." James began, taking an awkward step back from Saint-Germain.

"And you must learn to . . . survive."

"*NO!*" He flung himself away from le Comte, bringing his arms up to shield his face as if from blows.

"Mister Tree . . ."

"It's *crazy!*" With an inarticulate cry, he rushed toward the door.

Before he could reach it, Saint-Germain had moved with remarkable speed and blocked James's path. "Sit down, Mister Tree."

"I . . ." James said, raising one hand to threaten the smaller man.

"I would advise against it, Mister Tree," Saint-Germain warned him gently, with a trace of humor in his expression that baffled James anew. "Sit down."

The impetus which had driven James to action left him as quickly as it had possessed him and he permitted himself to be pointed in the direction of the chair he had just vacated. He told himself that he was in the presence of a lunatic and that he ought to go along with him; but deeper in his mind was the gnawing fear that, against all reason, Saint-Germain might be right. He moved stiffly and, as he sat down, he drew back into the chair as if to protect himself. "You're . . ."

"I'm not going to hurt you, if that is what concerns you," Saint-Germain sighed. When James did not deny his fear, Saint-Germain crossed the room away from him and regarded him for two intolerably long minutes. "Madelaine loves you, Mister Tree, and for that alone, I would offer you my assistance."

"You were her lover once, if you're who I think you are." He had summoned a little defiance into his accusation.

"I have told you so. Yes, she and I were lovers, as you and she were." There was an eighteenth-century lowboy against the wall, and Saint-Germain braced himself against it, studying James as he did.

"And you're not jealous?" James fairly pounced on the words.

"In time, we learn to bow to the inevitable. My love for Madelaine has not diminished, Mister Tree, but for those of our nature, such contact is . . . shall we say, nonproductive?" His tone was sardonic; his face was sad. "No, I am not jealous."

James heard this out in disbelief. "You want me to believe that?"

"I would prefer that you did," Saint-Germain said, then shrugged. "You will discover it for yourself, in time."

"Because I'm a vampire, like you two, right?" The sarcasm James had intended to convey was not entirely successful.

"Yes."

"Christ." James scowled, then looked up. "I said, 'Christ.' If I'm a vampire, how come I can do that? I thought all vampires were supposed to blanche and cringe at holy words and symbols." He was not enjoying himself, but asking this question made him feel more comfortable, as if the world were sane again.

"You will find that there are a great many misconceptions about us, Mister Tree. One of them is that we are diabolic. Would you be reassured if I could not say God, or Jesus, or Holy Mary, Mother of God? Give me a crucifix and I will kiss it, or a rosary and I will recite the prayers. I will read from the Torah, the Koran, the Vedas, or any other sacred literature you prefer. There is a Bible in the library—shall I fetch it, so that you may put your mind at rest?" He did not conceal his exasperation, but he mitigated his outburst with a brief crack of laughter.

"This is absurd," James said uncertainly.

Saint-Germain came a few steps closer. "Mister Tree, when you accepted Madelaine as your mistress, you knew that she was not entirely like other women. At the time, I would imagine that lent a thrill to what you did. No, don't bristle at me. I'm not implying that your passion was not genuine: if it was not, you would not have been given her love as you have." He fingered the lapel of his jacket. "This is rather awkward for me."

"I can see why," James said, feeling a greater degree of confidence. "If you keep telling me about . . ."

"It's awkward because I know how you love Madelaine—and she you. And how I love her—and she me." He read the puzzled look that James banished swiftly. "You will not want to relinquish what you have had, but . . ."

"Because you're back, is that it?" James challenged, sitting straight in the overstuffed chair.

"No. After all, Madelaine is on a dig, so her choice—if one were possible—is a moot point at best. I am afraid that it is more far-reaching than that." He came back to his chair, but though he rested one arm across the back, he did not sit. "For the sake of argument, Mister Tree, accept for the moment that you have been killed and are now a vampire."

James chuckled. "All right, I'm a vampire. But according to you, so is Madelaine, as well as you."

"Among vampires," Saint-Germain went on, not responding to James's provocation, "there is a most abiding love. Think of how the change was accomplished, and you will perceive why this is so. But once we come into our life, the expression of that love . . . changes, as well. We hunger for life, Mister Tree. And that is the one thing we cannot offer one another."

"Oh crap," James burst out. "I don't know how much of this I can listen to."

Saint-Germain's manner became more steely. "You will listen to it all, Mister Tree, or you will come to regret it." He waited until James settled back into the chair once again. "As I have told you," he resumed in the same even tone, "you will have to learn to seek out those who will respond to . . . what you can offer. For we do offer a great deal to those we love, Mister Tree. You know how profoundly intimate your love is for Madelaine. That is what you will have to learn to give to others if you are to survive."

"Life through sex?" James scoffed feebly. "Freud would love it."

Though Saint-Germain's fine brows flicked together in annoyance, he went on with hardly a pause. "Yes, through, if you take that to mean a route. Sex is not what you must strive for, but true intimacy. Sex is often a means to avoid intimacy—hardly more than the scratching of an itch. But when the act is truly intimate, there is no more intense experience, and that, Mister Tree, is what you must achieve." He cocked his head to the side. "Tell me: when you were with Madelaine, how did you feel?"

The skepticism went out of James's eyes and his face softened. "I wish I could tell you. I can't begin to express it. No one else ever . . ."

"Yes," Saint-Germain agreed rather sadly. "You will do well to remember it, in future."

On the hearth one of the logs crackled and burst, filling the room with the heavy scent of pine resin. A cascade of sparks flew onto the stone flooring and died as they landed.

James swallowed and turned away from Saint-Germain. He wanted to find a rational, logical objection to throw back at the black-clad man to dispell the dread that was filling him, the gnawing certainty that he was being told the truth. "I don't believe it," he whispered.

Saint-Germain had seen this shock so many times that he was no longer distressed by it, but merely saddened. He approached James and looked down at him. "You will have to accept it, Mister Tree, or you will have to die the true death. Madelaine would mourn for you terribly if you did that."

"'Die the true death.'" James bit his lower lip. "How . . ."

"Anything that destroys the nervous system destroys us: fire, crushing, beheading, or the traditional stake through the heart, for that matter, which breaks the spine. If you choose to die, there are many ways to do it." He said it matter-of-factly enough, but there was something at the back of his eyes that made James wonder how many times Saint-Germain had found himself regretting losses of those who had not learned to live as he claimed they must.

"And drowning? Isn't water supposed to . . ." James was amazed to hear this question. He had tried to keep from giving the man any credence and now he was reacting as if everything he heard was sensible.

"You will learn to line the heels and soles of your shoes with your native earth and you will cross water, walk in sunlight, in fact live a fairly normal life. We are creatures of the earth, Mister Tree. That which interrupts our contact with it is debilitating. Water is the worst, of course, but flying in an airplane is . . . unnerving." He had traveled by air several times, but had not been able to forget the huge distance between him and the treasured earth. "It will be more and more the way we travel—Madelaine says that she has gotten used to it but does not enjoy it—but I must be old-fashioned; I don't like it, although it is preferable to sailing, for brevity if nothing else."

"You make it sound so mundane," James said in the silence that fell. That alone was persuading him, and for that reason, he tried to mock it.

"Most of life is mundane, even our life." He smiled, and for the first time, there was warmth in it. "We are not excused from the obligations of living, unless we live as total outcasts. Some of us have, but such tactics are . . . unrewarding."

"Maybe not death, but taxes?" James suggested with an unhappy chuckle.

Saint-Germain gave James a sharp look. "If you wish to think of it in that way, it will answer fairly well," he said after a second or two. "If you live in the world, there are accommodations that must be made."

"This is bizarre," James said, convincing himself that he was amused while the unsettling apprehension grew in him steadily.

"When you came here," Saint-Germain continued, taking another line of argument, "when did you travel?"

"What?" James made an abrupt gesture with his hand, as if to push something away. "I didn't look about for public transportation, so I can't tell you what time . . ."

"Day or night will do," Saint-Germain said.

"Why, it was da . . ." His face paled. "No. I . . . passed out during the day. I decided it was safer at night, in any case. There are fewer patrols and . . ."

"When did you decide this? Before or after you had walked the better part of one night?" He let James have all the time he wanted to answer the question.

"I walked at night," James said in a strange tone. "The first night it was . . . easier. And I was so exhausted that I wasn't able to move until sundown. That night, with the moon so full, and seeing so well, I figured I might as well take advantage of it . . ."

"Mister Tree, the moon is not full, nor was it two nights ago. It is in its first quarter." He was prepared to defend this, but he read James's troubled face and did not press his argument. "Those who have changed see very well at night. You may, in fact, want to avoid bright sunlight, for our eyes are sensitive. We also gain strength and stamina. How else do you suppose you covered the distance you did with the sorts of wounds you sustained to slow you down?"

"I . . . I didn't think about it," he answered softly. "It was . . . natural."

"For those . . ."

". . . who have changed, don't tell me!" James burst out and lurched out of the chair. "If you keep this up, you'll have me believing it, and then I'll start looking for a padded cell and the latest thing in straitjackets." He paced the length of the room once, coming back to stand near Saint-Germain. "You're a smooth-tongued bastard, I'll give you that, Saint-Germain. You *are* Saint-Germain, aren't you?"

"Of course. I thought you remembered me from that banquet in Paris," came the unperturbed answer.

"I did. But I thought you'd look . . ."

"Older?" Saint-Germain suggested. "When has Madelaine looked older than twenty? True, you have not seen her for more than six years, but when she came to America, did she strike you as being older than the day you met her?"

"No," James admitted.

"And she looks very little older now than she did the day I met her in 1743. You are fortunate that age has been kind to you, Mister Tree. That is one of the few things the change cannot alter." Abruptly he crossed the room and opened the door. "I trust you will give me an hour of your time later this evening. Roger should be back by then and then you will have a chance to . . ."

"Has he gone for food?" James demanded, not wanting to admit he was famished.

"Something like that," le Comte answered, then stepped into the hall and pulled the door closed behind him.

The Bugatti pulled into the court behind the stables and, in a moment, Roger had turned off the foglights and the ignition. He motioned to the woman beside him, saying, "I will get your bag, Madame, and then assist you."

"Thank you," the woman answered distantly. She was not French, though she spoke the language well. Her clothes, which were excellent quality, hung on her shapelessly, and the heavy circles under her eyes and the hollows at her throat showed that she had recently suffered more than the usual privations of war. Automatically she put her hand to her forehead, as if to still an ache there.

"Are you all right, Madame?" Roger asked as he opened the passenger door for her. In his left hand he held a single, worn leather valise.

"I will be, in a short time," she responded, unable to smile, but knowing that good manners required something of the sort from her.

Roger offered her his arm. "You need not feel compelled, Madame. If, on reflection, the matter we discussed is distasteful to you, tell me at once, and I . . ." He turned in relief as he saw Saint-Germain approaching through the night.

"You're back sooner than I expected," Saint-Germain said with an inquiring lift to his brows.

"I had an unexpected opportunity," was the answer. "Just as well, too, because there are Resistance fighters gathering further down the mountain, and they do not take kindly to travelers."

"I see," Saint-Germain responded.

"A number of them wished to . . . detain Madame Kunst, hearing her speak . . . and . . ." Roger chose his words carefully.

"I am Austrian," the woman announced a bit too loudly. "I *am*. I fled." Without warning, she started to cry with the hopelessness of an abandoned child. "They took my mother and my father and shot them," she said through her tears. "And then they killed my uncle and his three children. They wanted me, but I was shopping. A neighbor warned me. It wasn't enough that Gunther died for defending his friends, oh no."

Saint-Germain motioned Roger aside, then held out his small beautiful hand to Madame Kunst. "Come inside, Madame Kunst. There is a fire and food."

She sat passively while her tears stopped, then obediently took his hand, and for the first time looked into Saint-Germain's penetrating eyes. "Danke, Mein Herr."

"It would be wiser to say 'merci' here," Saint-Germain reminded her kindly. "My experience with the Resistance in this area says they are not very forgiving."

"Yes. I was stupid," she said as she got out of the Bugatti and allowed Saint-Germain to close the door. In an effort to recapture her poise, she said, "Your manservant made a request of me as he brought me here."

Roger and Saint-Germain exchanged quick glances, and Saint-Germain hesitated before saying, "You must understand, this is not precisely the situation I had anticipated. Did my manservant explain the situation to you clearly? I do not want to ask you to do anything you think you would not wish to do."

She shrugged, shaking her head once or twice. "It doesn't matter to me. Or it does, but it makes no sense."

"How do you mean?" Saint-Germain had seen this lethargic shock many times in the past, but long familiarity did not make it easier to bear. He would have to make other arrangements for

James, he thought; this woman clearly needed quiet and time to restore herself. She had had more than enough impositions on her.

"It's all so . . ." She sighed as Saint-Germain opened the side door for her and indicated the way into the château. "No man has touched me since Gunther, and I was content to be in my father's house, where the worst seemed so far away. When I thought those men might force me, I screamed, but there was no reason for it anymore."

"You have nothing to fear from anyone at Montalia," Saint-Germain told her quietly.

She nodded and let Roger escort her into the breakfast room off the kitchen. There was a low fire in the grate and though the striped wallpaper was faded, in the flickering light it was pleasant and cozy. As Saint-Germain closed the door, she sat in the chair Roger held for her and folded her hands in her lap. Her age was no more than thirty, but the gesture was that of a much younger person. "Gunther died six months ago. I didn't find out about it at first. They don't tell you what's happened. The SS comes and people go out with them and don't come home again—and no one dares ask where they have gone, or when they will return, for then the SS might return. It was the local judge who told me—and he was drunk when he did."

Roger bowed and excused himself to prepare a simple meal for Madame Kunst.

"When did you leave Austria, Madame?" Saint-Germain asked her as he added another log to the fire.

"Not many days. Eight or nine, I think. It could be ten." She yawned and apologized.

"There is no need," Saint-Germain assured her. "The fare here is adequate but not luxurious. If you are able to wait half an hour, there will be soup and cheese and sausage. Perhaps you would like to nap in the meantime?"

She thought about this, then shook her head. "I would sleep like the dead. I must stay awake. There are too many dead already." She fiddled with the fold of her skirt across her lap, but her mind was most certainly drifting. "I ate yesterday."

Saint-Germain said nothing, but he could not repress an ironic smile, and was relieved that he had attended to his own hunger a

few days before. The matter of nourishment, he thought, was becoming ridiculously complex.

"You did *what?*" James exclaimed, outraged. He had come
back to the sitting room some ten minutes before and had tried to
listen in reserved silence to what Saint-Germain was telling him.

"I saw that she was fed and given a room. I'm sorry that this
adds so many complications. Had Roger been able to reach
Mirelle, the problem would not have arisen." He was unruffled by
James's outburst.

"*First,* you send your valet out to get a cooperative widow for
me, and when that doesn't work because he can't get through to
the village, he brings a half-starved Austrian refugee here as a
weird kind of substitute, never mind what the poor woman thinks,
being half-kidnapped. *Second,* you think I'll go along with this impossible scheme. *Third,* you're telling me that you bring women
here the way some cooks rustle up a half a dozen eggs and I'm
supposed to be grateful?" His voice had risen to a shout, as much
to conceal the guilty pleasure he felt at the prospect of so tantaliz-
ing a meeting.

"Mister Tree, if there were not a war going on, all this would
be handled differently. It may surprise you to know that I am not
in the habit of 'rustling up,' as you say, cooperative widows or
anyone else, for that matter. However, your situation will be critical soon if something is not done, and I had hoped to find as un-
disruptive a solution as possible."

"Well, you sure as hell botched it," James said, taking secret
pleasure in seeing this elegant stranger at a loss.

"Lamentably, I must concur." He thrust his hands into his
pockets and started toward the door.

James could not resist a parting shot. "You mean you were
going to lay out a woman for me, like a smorgasbord, so I
could . . ."

Saint-Germain's mobile lips turned down in disgust. "What do
you take me for, Mister Tree? Mirelle knows what I am and finds
it most satisfying. She would enjoy the . . . variety you would
offer her. Good God, you don't believe that I would expose a
woman like Madame Kunst to what we are, do you? She under-

stands there is a man here suffering from battle fatigue, and is prepared to make allowances. It is dangerous and unwise to spend time with those who are repelled by us. If you are to survive in this life, you must learn to be circumspect." He reached for the door, then added, "Roger found the two boxes of earth from Denver, and that will afford you some relief, but not, I fear, a great deal."

"Earth from Denver?" James echoed.

"Of course. When Madelaine knew that you would walk after death, she arranged to have two cartons of your native earth shipped here, in case it was needed." It was said lightly, but the significance did not escape James. "She had stored it in the stables, and Roger did not find it until late afternoon."

"Earth from Denver. I can't believe it." There would have been comfort and denial in laughter, but James could not summon any.

"She cares what happens to you, Mister Tree. It was not whim but concern for your welfare that made her get those two boxes." He opened the door wide and stepped into the hall. His face was clouded with thought and he made his way slowly to the kitchen.

Roger looked up as Saint-Germain came quietly through the door. "She's bathed and gone to bed."

"Good. Did you learn anything more?" He was frowning slightly; there was an indefinable restlessness about him.

"Nothing significant. She's twenty-nine, comes from Salzburg. She used to teach school; her husband . . ."

"Gunther?"

"Yes. He was an attorney, I gather." He finished tidying the clutter in the kitchen and turned to bank the coals in the huge wood-burning stove.

"Do you believe her?" Saint-Germain asked quietly.

"That she was a teacher and her husband an attorney, yes. The rest, I don't know." Roger closed the fuel box and wiped his hands on a rag, leaving blackened smudges on the worn cloth.

"Nor do I," Saint-Germain admitted. "It may only be shock, but. . . . But."

Roger blew out one of the kerosene lanterns. "Is she what she seems?"

"Superficially, no doubt," Saint-Germain said measuredly.

"And everything she has told us may be true. If that's the case, she might be blackmailed. If she has children, and they are held by the SS, she might undertake almost anything to save them. Because if she is what she claims to be and she wants to be out of Austria and away from the war, why didn't she stop in Switzerland? That's a neutral country."

"She might not feel safe there," Roger suggested.

"And instead she feels safe in France?" Saint-Germain countered in disbelief. "You know what the French want to do to the Germans these days. Why should she leave the comparative haven Switzerland offers for this?"

"Is it espionage?" Roger asked, taking the other lantern and starting toward the door.

"We will doubtless soon find out. But we must be very cautious. All the Resistance would need is an excuse to come here hunting German spies and matters might suddenly become unpleasant for us." He accompanied Roger out of the kitchen and toward the tower, the oldest part of the château. "I'm afraid I've scandalized Mister Tree again," Saint-Germain remarked as the reverberations of their footsteps clattered away into the eerie darkness. "He's accused me of pimping."

Roger gave a snort of amusement. "How charming. Did he say it directly?"

"Not quite. That would mean he would have to see too clearly what has become of him. It is unfortunate that you did not reach Mirelle. She would have put an end to all this nonsense and the worst of his anxiety would be over by now. He's badly frightened; the thing that could not possibly happen to him has happened. Mirelle would tease him out of it. It's a pity she does not want to be one of my blood in the end. She would do well." They reached a narrow, uneven stairway that led into the upper rooms of the tower, and Saint-Germain stood aside for Roger so that he could light his way. The lantern was unnecessary for Saint-Germain, but his manservant required more illumination.

"It's best that she should know her mind now," Roger said, picking his way up the hazardous stairs. "Later, it might be inconvenient."

"True enough," Saint-Germain murmured. "Which room are the boxes in?"

"The second, where the trunks are stored. I stumbled on them by chance." They were halfway up the stairs now, and Roger paid particular attention to this stretch, for he knew that the one short trip stair was located here.

"To hide a box, put it with other boxes," Saint-Germain said, paraphrasing the maxim. "I have always applauded Madelaine's cleverness."

Roger got past the trip stair and moved faster. "Both boxes are unmarked, but there is the stencil design of an oak on both of them, which was what alerted me."

"How very like her," le Comte chuckled. They were almost at the landing, and he smiled his anticipation. "He'll be more at ease with this."

"Perhaps, perhaps not," Roger responded with a shrug. On the landing, he pointed to the door. "That one. There's a stack of boxes in the north corner. They're on the top of it."

As he opened the door and stepped into the room, Saint-Germain said over his shoulder, "You know, it is inconvenient that our scars can't be altered. Plastic surgery might change any number of things. Mister Tree is going to have some distinctive marks on his arms and thighs that will make identification simple. If there were a way to remove them, it might be easier to go from alias to alias. Well, that time may come." He looked around for the stack Roger had described. "Ah. There. If you'll give me a hand getting them down, I will take them to Mister Tree's room."

James woke at sunset feeling more restored than he had since his accident. He stretched slowly, oddly pleased that there were no aches to hamper his movements. He was healing, he insisted to himself. When he rose from the bed, there was the first hint of an energetic spring in his step. He dressed carefully, noticing that his clothes had been pressed sometime during the day. The only things that he could not find were his shoes. After a brief hunt for them, he shrugged and settled for a pair of heavy boots he had worn years before when he and Madelaine had gone tramping over the rough hillsides together. As he laced them up, he thought how comfortable they were and hoped that le Comte would not be too offended by them.

When at last he ventured down to the sitting room, he found Madame Kunst finishing the last of her tea, a few crumbs left on the Limoges plate beside her cup and saucer. He hesitated, then came into the room. "Good afternoon."

She looked up suddenly, guiltily, then smiled as best she could. "Good afternoon, though it is more evening, I think. You are . . ."

"The American suffering from battle fatigue, yes," he said with the same directness he had used to disarm politicians and industrialists for more than two decades. "You needn't worry, Madame. I am not precisely out of control, as you can see." To demonstrate this, he took a chair and arranged himself casually in it.

"I'm glad you're feeling . . . better?" This last change of inflection caught his attention and he leaned forward to speak to her.

"Yes. I'm much revived, thanks." He had deliberately chosen a chair that was far enough away from her that she would not be too much disturbed by his presence.

"You're an officer?" she asked when she had poured herself another cup of tea. She pointed to the pot in mute invitation, saying, "If you like, I could ring for another cup."

"That would be . . ." He broke off, finding the thought of tea distasteful. "Very good of you, but it would be wasted on me," he finished, frowning a bit.

"Is anything the matter?" she inquired apprehensively.

"No, not really." He decided to answer her question. "I'm not an officer, or a soldier, I'm afraid. I'm a journalist. I've been covering the action toward Lyons, but it hasn't been what I expected."

Madame Kunst smiled politely. "I'd think not." She sipped her tea. "What is your impression? Or would you rather not discuss it?"

"You must know the answer to that better than I," James suggested blandly, the habits of caution exerting themselves.

"Only what we are told," she said with a degree of sadness.

"But there must be raids and . . ." he said, hoping she would take up his drift.

"We hear about them, naturally, but Salzburg is not as important as other places. It is not important to shipping or the offensive, so we do not know how the rest of the country is going on." She finished the tea and reluctantly set the cup aside. "They have real butter here, and the milk is fresh."

The mention of food made James queasy, but he was able to nod. "Yes. There are shortages everywhere. Back home, there are ration cards used for meat and other necessary items. The government encourages everyone to grow their own vegetables." He knew it was safe to mention this, because it was common knowledge and there were articles in the newspapers which any enemy spy who wished to could read.

"There isn't much opportunity to grow vegetables in a city flat," she said.

"True enough. I have a cousin who always sends me canned goods at Christmas. She has quite a garden and thinks I need her food." He wanted to get off the subject, but did not quite know how.

Madame Kunst spared him the trouble. "How long have you been in France, Herr . . . ? I believe I was not told your name."

This time he could not avoid giving his name. "Tree, Madame Kunst. You see, I have been told who you are. I'm James Emmerson Tree. I've been in France a little more than a year."

"So long, with the war and all." She waited patiently for him to answer.

"Reporters go where the story is, and this is the biggest story around," he said with a shrug that did not completely conceal his disillusion with his work. "I'd been in France before, in the Twenties, and it made me the logical candidate to come back to cover this." He ran his hand through his hair. "You'll have to forgive me, Madame Kunst. I must be disconcerting company. These clothes aren't the latest; I haven't done anything much about my hair or shaving, but don't be alarmed." He touched his chin tentatively and felt a slight roughness, as if he had shaved the evening before.

"We do what we can in these times," she said, trying to appear at her best. "I have two dresses—and the other is worse than this one."

There was a tap at the door, and then Roger entered. "Excuse me, Madame Kunst, but if you are finished with your tea, I will remove the tray for you."

"Yes, I am, thank you," she replied, a trifle more grandly than she had addressed James. "It was very good."

"There will be a supper in two or three hours. Served in the breakfast room, as it is easiest to heat." He picked up the tray and started toward the door. "Mister Tree, le Comte would appreciate it if you could spare him a moment of your time."

James scowled. "When?"

"At your convenience. In the next two hours, perhaps?" He gave a little bow and left the room.

"My aunt had a butler like that, years ago," Madame Kunst said wistfully when Roger had gone.

"He's very efficient," James admitted grudgingly, deciding that Roger was a bit *too* efficient.

"Servants aren't like that anymore." She smoothed the skirt of her dress and looked over at James. "How did you find the situation in France when you arrived?"

"Chaotic," James answered. "It's apparent that this war has taken a dreadful toll on the country."

"On all Europe," Madame Kunst corrected him.

"Sure. But I've been covering France, and this is where I've had to look for the damage, the ruin, and the destruction. I've heard about conditions in Russia and I'm appalled. Italy is supposed to be having very bad troubles, and the Netherlands and Scandinavia are suffering, too, but France, in many ways, is taking the brunt of it. When I was in London, I was shocked, but when I came to France, I was horrified." He sensed that he was talking too much, but was no longer able to stop himself. "The First World War was ruinous, but this is something a lot worse. And the rumors we keep hearing make it all sound a lot worse than we think it is. There's nothing as bad as trench warfare going on, and no mounted cavalry against tanks, as there was before, but the cities are burning and the country is laid waste, and there doesn't seem to be any end in sight. What can anyone think? It can't go on endlessly, but there is no way to end it."

"At home, we all pray that it will end," she said softly, her large brown eyes turned appealingly toward him. "Don't you think the Americans could do something? If your President would insist that we stop, all of us at once, then it could not go on. Without the Americans, the British and the French could not continue this insanity."

"The Americans don't see it that way, Madame Kunst," James said rather stiffly, feeling disturbed by her afresh.

"But what are we to do if it goes on and on? Everyone in my family is dead but myself, and no one cares that this is the case. Down the street from where my family lived, there is a widow who had lost four sons—all of them flyers killed in air battles. She is like a ghost in her house. And there are hundreds, thousands like her."

"As there are in France and Italy and England and Holland, Madame Kunst. As there are in Chicago and Montreal and Honolulu." He got up. "Excuse me, but it might be best if I talk to le Comte now, rather than later."

Her face changed. "Have I offended you? Please, don't think me heartless or uncaring of the sufferings of others. That is why I spoke to you about a resolution to this terrible war, so that there need not be such women ever again."

"I'm not offended," James said, knowing that he was and was uncertain why. As he left the room, he passed near her chair, and for one moment, he was caught and held by the sound of her pulse.

"She gave me a lecture on pacifism," James said at last when Saint-Germain had asked him for a third time what he and Madame Kunst had found to talk about. "She wants me to end the war so no more widows will lose sons. God knows, I don't want to see any more deaths, but what's the alternative?"

"Capitulation?" Saint-Germain suggested.

"Oh no. You've seen the way the Germans have treated every foot of land they've taken. And they say there's worse things going on. One of the Dutch reporters said that there were cattle cars full of people being taken away. If they're doing that in Germany to Germans, what would they do to the rest of us." He gestured once. "That could be propaganda about the cattle cars, but if it isn't . . ."

"I do see your point, Mister Tree. I am not convinced that you see mine. Montalia is isolated and splendidly defensible. A person here, or in one of the houses in, shall we say, a ten-kilometer radius, with a radio receiver and a reasonable amount of prudence, might provide the Germans with extremely useful information." He watched James as he said this, expecting an argument.

"But what good would it be?" James objected, taking his favorite role of devil's advocate. "You said yourself that the château is isolated, and God knows, this part of Provence is damned remote. What could anyone find out here? There's nothing very strategic in your ten-kilometer radius unless you think that they're going to start last-ditch battles for the smaller passes."

"We're very close to Switzerland. As many secrets as gold are brokered through Geneva and Zurich. With a listening post here, a great deal could be learned." Saint-Germain raised one shoulder. "I may be feinting at shadows, but it worries me."

"If they want a listening post for Switzerland, why not *in* Switzerland?" James asked.

"The Swiss take a dim view of the abuse of their neutrality. Certainly there are monitoring posts in Bavaria and Austria, but it is not as easy to watch Geneva and Lausanne. The Resistance have found men and women doing espionage work in these mountains before. Last year, it was a gentleman claiming to be a naturalist hoping to preserve a particular bird; he climbed all over the mountains and stayed in the old monastery on the next ridge. He might have accomplished his task, whatever it was, if one of the Resistance men did not become suspicious when he saw the supposed naturalist walk by a nest of the bird in question without a second look. It may be that Madame Kunst is nothing more than an Austrian refugee in a panic, but I am not going to assume anything until she has shown me I have no reason to be concerned."

James chuckled. "And where do you fit into this?"

"I don't want to fit into it at all," was Saint-Germain's short rejoinder. "War ceased to amuse me millen . . . years ago." He shook his head. "Apparently you haven't considered our position. We are both foreigners in a country at war. If we are imprisoned, which could happen—it has happened before—our particular needs would make a prolonged stay . . . difficult." He recalled several of the times he had been confined and each brought its own burden of revulsion. "You would not like prison, Mister Tree."

"I wouldn't like it in any case," James said at once. "I knew a reporter who was shot by the Spanish for trying to file an uncensored story. He'd done it before and they caught him trying the same thing again."

Saint-Germain lifted his head and listened. "Ah. That will be Mirelle. We will continue this at a later time, Mister Tree."

"What?" James cried, remembering the woman's name all too clearly. Now he, too, could hear an approaching automobile.

"You do have need of her, Mister Tree," Saint-Germain said quietly. "More than you know now."

James came off the sofa to round on le Comte. "It's monstrous. I've gone along with some of what you've told me, but I draw the line at this!"

"Perhaps you should wait until you have a better idea of what 'this' is," Saint-Germain said, a touch of his wry humor returning. "She is looking forward to this evening. It would be sad if you were to disappoint her."

"Come on," James protested.

This time, when Saint-Germain spoke, his voice was low and his eyes compassionate. "Mister Tree, you will have to learn sometime, and we haven't the luxury of leisure. Mirelle wants to have the pleasure of taking your vampiric virginity, and you would do well to agree. We are rarely so fortunate in our first . . . experiences. You will spare yourself a great deal of unpleasantness if you will set aside your worry and pride long enough to lie with her. Believe this."

"But . . ." James began, then stopped. He could feel his hunger coiled within him, and he knew without doubt that it was hearing the beat of Madame Kunst's heart that had sharpened it. "Okay, I'll try. If nothing else," he went on with a poor attempt at jauntiness, "I'll get a good lay."

Saint-Germain's brows rose. "It is essential that *she* have the . . . good lay. Otherwise you will have nothing, Mister Tree. Males of our blood are like this." He was about to go on when there was a quick, emphatic step in the hall and the door was flung open.

Mirelle Bec was thirty-four, firm-bodied, and comfortably voluptuous. She did not so much enter the room as burst into it with profligate vitality. Drab clothes and lack of cosmetics could not disguise her sensuality. Her hair was a dark cloud around a pert face that was more exciting than pretty—and when she spoke, it was in rapid, enthusiastic bursts. "Comte!" she called out and hastened across the room to fling her arms around him. "You've kept away so long, I ought to be annoyed with you, but I could never do that."

Saint-Germain kissed her cheek affectionately. "I have missed seeing you too, Mirelle."

As she disengaged herself from his embrace, she pointed dramatically at James. "Is *this* the baby? Comte, you are a bad, bad man. You did not tell me he was so beautiful." To James's embarrassment, Mirelle gave him a thorough and very appraising looking over. "Oh, this is very promising," she declared as she approached him. "I do like the white hair. It is distinguished, is it not?" As James tried not to squirm, she laughed aloud and reached for his hand. "You are shy? But how delightful." Over her shoulder, she added to Saint-Germain, "How good of you to offer him to me. I am going to enjoy myself tremendously."

"But, Madame, we . . ." James said in confusion, trying to find some way to deal with her.

"Have not been introduced, is that what concerns you? I am Mirelle, and you, I have been told, are James. So. We are introduced now. It remains only for you to show me which room is yours."

James had had experience with many women, but this one took him wholly aback. Yet even as he tried to separate himself from her, he felt the draw of her and his much-denied hunger responded to her. "Madame . . ."

"No, no, no. Mirelle. You are James. I am Mirelle. It is more friendly that way, is it not?" She drew his arm through hers. "You will tell me how you come to be here as we walk to your room."

"I am not sure that . . ." James began with a look of mute appeal to Saint-Germain which he studiously avoided.

"But I am. Let us go, James." She waved to le Comte and went quickly to the door, taking the ambivalent James with her.

"Christ, I'm sorry," James muttered sometime later. They were in a glorious tangle on his bed, with the covers in complete disarray. "If you give me a little time, Mirelle. . . . I must be more worn out than I knew."

Mirelle gave a sympathetic laugh. "It is not fatigue, James; it is what you are." She trailed her fingers over his chest. "Weren't you told?"

"I've been told all kinds of things the last couple days," he sighed in disgust.

"But this—this is different," Mirelle said generously. "For a man, this is more important, is it not?" She snuggled closer to him, pressing her body to his. "It is not the same when one changes. But there are compensations."

"For this? I've never been impotent before," James said, a note of distress creeping into his voice.

"It is not impotent," Mirelle assured him. "You are more than ready to make love to me, yes? And you are not repelled by me. So this is another matter."

"You don't know what it is that I . . . almost did." He felt suddenly miserable; he wanted to shut out the drumming of her heart that was loud as heavy machinery in his ears.

Mirelle laughed deeply. "But of course I know what you almost did. You are the same as le Comte. You wanted to put your lips to my neck and taste . . ."

"For God's sake!" James interrupted her, trying to move away from her but not succeeding.

"Well," Mirelle said reasonably, "it is what I expected of you. But you have not entirely got the way of it. You are judging yourself by your earlier standards—and they do not apply, my cabbage."

James rolled onto his side and rested his hand on the rise of Mirelle's hip. "Look, you're being very nice about this and I appreciate it, but . . ." He wanted to shrug the incident off, to promise her another hour when he was feeling a bit better, but he could not find a gracious way to do so. He loved the feel of her skin under his hand and her nearness was oddly intoxicating, so that he could not bring himself to leave the bed or ask her to leave it.

"You are discouraged, but you need not be, James. You have not gotten used to your new ways. You don't have to worry. Let me show you. I love showing." Her hazel eyes took on a greenish shine of mischief. "You must learn how to satisfy me. It is not too difficult, ami, and when it is done, you will do well enough for yourself." She wriggled expertly. "Now, your hand *there,* if you please. That is a good beginning."

Dazed, James did as he was told, letting her instruct him as if he were a boy of fourteen. At first, he could not get the memory of the long nights with Madelaine out of his thoughts, but then, as his passion grew in answer to Mirelle's, he responded to her, and only to her, and this time, though he did not love her as he had supposed he would, he had no reason to apologize.

Roger escorted Madame Kunst to her room, and listened quietly to her protestations that she was reluctant to remain at Montalia. "I have those I wish to meet. It isn't wise for me to remain here."

"But there is fighting, Madame, and you would not be safe, should you venture out into the world as it is now." Roger had received Saint-Germain's instructions several hours before to be solicitous of the Austrian woman.

"They said that there would be a boat at Nice that would take me to Scotland. I must reach that boat. I must."

"My master will make inquiries on your behalf, Madame. It would not be pleasant for you to suffer any more mishaps." Roger was unfailingly polite and slightly deferent, but gave no indication that he would accommodate her.

"He has some influence, this Comte? Could he help me?" Her voice pleaded, but her wary eyes were hard.

"That is for him to decide, Madame Kunst. I will mention what you have told me." The hallway was dark where the glow of the lantern did not shine. "You have enough candles in your room?"

"There are plenty, thank you," she answered abruptly. Again

she grasped the handle. "I must leave. I must go to Scotland. Can you explain that?"

"I will tell my master what you have said."

Her hands came up to her chin in fists. "Oh, you stupid man!" she shouted in her frustration, and then was at once quiet and restrained. "Forgive me. I must be more . . . tired than I realize."

"Of course, Madame Kunst." He lifted the lantern higher. "You can see your way?"

She did not entirely take the hint. "That woman," she said as she paused on the threshold. "I suppose she is necessary?"

Roger gave her no response whatever and there was a subtle sternness about his mouth that indicated he would not indulge in speculation about his master or Mirelle Bec.

"Well, such things happen, I suppose." She gave a polite shrug to show it made no difference to her if those in the house wanted to be immoral. "The highborn live by their own rules, do they not?"

"Good night, Madame Kunst," Roger said, and stepped back from her doorway. When he was satisfied that the door was firmly closed, he turned away from it and made his way back toward the sitting room where he knew that Saint-Germain waited for him. His sandy head was bent in thought and his face was not readable.

Shortly before sunrise, Saint-Germain found James walking in the overgrown garden. He came up to the American silently and fell into step beside him, letting James choose the path they were to take.

"She showed me," James said after a long while.

"Ah."

Their feet, as they walked, crunched on the unraked gravel that led between the abandoned flower beds. James reached out and pulled a cluster of dried, faded blossoms off a trailing branch as it brushed his shoulder. "It wasn't what I expected." The paper-crisp husks of the flowers ran between his fingers and fell.

"But tolerable?" Saint-Germain inquired as if they were discussing nothing more important than the temperature of bath water.

"Oh yeah. Tolerable." He laughed once, self-consciously. "Tolerable."

Saint-Germain continued his unhurried stroll, but pointed out that the sun would be up in half an hour. "You are not used to the sun yet, Mister Tree. Until you are, it might be wisest to spend the day indoors, if not asleep."

"Uh huh." He turned back toward the château, saying with some awkwardness, "Mirelle told me she'd be back in three or four days. But she didn't . . . Oh Christ! this is difficult."

"She will be here for you, Mister Tree. My need is not great just now." He answered the unasked question easily, and sensed James's relief.

"That's what she hinted." James looked sharply at the shorter man. "Why? Is it because you're after that Austrian woman?"

"What an appalling notion! No, of course I'm not." He expressed his indignation lightly, but decided that he had better explain. "Oh, if I were determined to . . . use her, I could wait until she was asleep and visit her then and she would remember little more than a very pleasant dream. It is something we all learn to do in time and it has its advantages upon occasion. But Madame Kunst is a bit of a puzzle. Her purpose for being here is not known to me and it would not be sensible or wise to . . . be close to her. If she learned or guessed what I am, and wished me ill, she would have me at a distinct disadvantage. The Resistance might not mind taking off time from hunting Nazis and Nazi sympathizers to hunt a more old-fashioned menace. You must not forget that is how most of the world sees us—as menaces. I would not like to have to leave Montalia precipitously just now." There had been many times in the past when he had had to take sudden flight in order to save himself; it was not a thing he wished to do again. "We must be circumspect, James."

This was the first time Saint-Germain had addressed him by his Christian name and it startled him. "Why do you call me James? Is it because of Mirelle?"

"Don't be absurd." Saint-Germain's wry smile was clear in the advancing light.

"You've been calling me Mister Tree since I arrived here." The tone of his statement was stubborn and James was plainly waiting for an answer.

"And you have not been calling me anything at all," was Saint-Germain's mild reply.

James faltered. "It's that . . . I don't know what to call you."

"Is it." Saint-Germain gestured toward the side door that led into the pantry. "This is the quickest way."

As James was about to go in, there came the drone of planes overhead. He looked up, searching the sky, and at last, off to the north, saw a formation of shapes headed west. "I can't tell whose they are," he said quietly.

"American or British bombers back from their nighttime raids. They're keeping to the south of Paris, for reasons of caution." He held the door for James.

"This far south?" James wondered aloud, already stepping into the shadow of the doorway.

"It is possible, James. They have done it before. You have been here very little time, and until last night you were not paying much attention to the world around you." There was no rebuke in what he said, and he felt none.

"True enough," James allowed, and waited while Saint-Germain closed the door behind them and latched it. "Why bother?"

"The farmers around here are very insular, careful folk, like all French peasants. They respect and admire Madelaine because she is the Seigneur. Don't look so surprised, Mister Tree. Surely you can understand this. The peasants are proud of their estate and they are protective of Montalia. Most of them think it is a great misfortune that the line has passed through females for so long, but that makes them all the more determined to guard Madelaine. They know what she does—or part of it. They would beat their daughters senseless for taking lovers, but the Seigneurs are different—and her adventures provide them endless entertainment."

They had come into the kitchen, where Roger was cutting up a freshly killed chicken. He looked up from his task and regarded the two men quizzically. "I didn't know you were outside."

"James was taking the air and I was coming back from checking the gatehouse," Saint-Germain said. "You might want to purchase some eggs from the Widow Saejean. Her boy told Mirelle that times are hard for them just now."

Roger nodded. "This afternoon." He bent and sniffed the chicken. "They're not able to feed them as well as they did."

"We could purchase a few of ours now, if that would help," Saint-Germain suggested, but Roger shook his head.

"Better to buy them. If we bring chickens here, we won't be able to feed them much better than the rest do, and they would resent it. We are still the foreigners, and it would not take much to have them remember it." He began to cut up the bird with a long chef's knife, letting the weight of the heavy blade do much of the work.

"About Madame Kunst . . ." Saint-Germain prompted.

"Nothing more, my master. I have not been able to touch her valise, which is locked, in any case. But I do know that it is heavy, heavier than it ought to be, considering her story." Roger looked down at the chicken parts and smiled.

"Very good." Saint-Germain motioned to the American. "Come, James. Let's permit Roger to enjoy his breakfast in peace." He indicated the passage toward the main hall and waited for James to accompany him.

Once they were out of the kitchen, James said, "I don't mean to sound stupid, but I thought Roger was . . ."

"A vampire?" Saint-Germain finished for him. "No."

Apparently needing to explain himself, James went on. "It's only that you seem to be so . . . used to each other."

Saint-Germain turned toward the front reception room, where tall windows gave a view of the rising mountains behind the promontory where Montalia sat. "I did not say that he is . . . unchanged, simply that he is not a vampire. Do sit down, if you wish, and be at ease. No," Saint-Germain said, resuming his topic, "Roger is not like us, but he has died and recovered from it. You were right; we are old friends. We met some time ago in Rome."

"If he's died and . . . what is he?" James knew that he ought to be bothered by these revelations or admit he was in the company of madmen, but after his night with Mirelle, he could not bring himself to accuse Saint-Germain of anything.

"He is a ghoul," Saint-Germain responded matter-of-factly. He saw James blink. "Don't imagine him back there tearing that poor fowl's carcass to bits with his teeth. There is no reason for it. He eats neatly because it is easier and more pleasant. The only restrictions his state imposes on him is that the meat—for he only eats meat—be fresh-killed and raw."

James shuddered and looked away. "I see."

"I'm not certain of that," Saint-Germain said quietly.

Eager to change the subject, James asked, "Why was he trying to look at Madame Kunst's valise?"

"Because she guards it so zealously," he answered at once. "I am curious about a woman who says that she avoided arrest by being out shopping when the rest of her family were taken—and yet carries a large valise. Did she take it shopping with her? Then for what was she shopping? If she picked it up later, why that bag, rather than another? She says that she only has two dresses. Good. But where did they come from? Did she buy a dress while shopping and take it with her when she fled? Did she buy it later? If Roger says that the valise is heavy, then you may believe him. In that case, what is in it?"

"Maybe she went back to her house and grabbed the only valise she could find, stuffed clothes into it, and something of value, say, silver candlesticks, so that she could pay for her passage. She wants to go to Scotland, and I don't know if it would be safe to pay for her trip in marks." James turned the questions over in his mind as he answered, enjoying the process. "What if she got as far as Zurich, had to buy some clothes, but could only afford to buy a cheap valise? If she'd gone to the train . . ."

"And where did she get her travel permit?" Saint-Germain inquired evenly. "Whether she is going to Scotland or Poland, she would have to have the proper papers or she would not be able to get a ticket, let alone come this far."

"But if she didn't come by train? If she had a car . . ." He thought this over. "She would require proper documents to get over the border, that's true, and if her family was arrested, her name would probably be on a detain list."

"Yes. And where does that leave Madame Kunst?" With a shake of his head, Saint-Germain drew up a chair. "You are a journalist, James, and you are used to examining persons and facts. If the occasion should arise and you are able to draw out Madame Kunst, I would appreciate your evaluation. Don't force the issue, of course, because I don't want her alarmed. If she is truly nothing more than a refugee, determined—for reasons best known to herself—to get to Scotland, it would be a shame to cause her any more anguish. If she is not that, it would be foolish to put her on her guard."

"Are you always such a suspicious bastard?" James asked with increased respect.

"I am not suspicious at all. If I were, I should not have allowed her to come here. But I have seen enough treachery in my . . . life to wish to avoid it." He studied the tall American. "You would do well to develop a similar attitude, James. It spares us much inconvenience."

James gave this a reserved acceptance, then inquired, "What if she is an agent? What will you do then?"

"Inform the Resistance leaders. Yes, there are ways I can do this—and I will, if it is necessary. I hope that it is not; I do not want to live under constant surveillance, as I have told you before." He got up. "I have a few tasks to attend to. If you will excuse me?"

As he started toward the door, James called after him. "What tasks?"

Saint-Germain paused. "I like to spend some time in my laboratory each day. It's a bit makeshift, but better than nothing."

"Laboratory? What do you do there?" James was somewhat intrigued, for although he had no great interest in scientific experimentation, he was curious about how Saint-Germain occupied his time.

"I make gold, of course." With James's indulgent laughter ringing in his ears, Saint-Germain left the reception room.

That afternoon James discovered Madame Kunst to be a fairly good—if impatient—cardplayer. They had begun with cribbage and had graduated to whist. As Madame Kunst put down her cards, she said, "After I have my supper, let us play another rubber. You have some skill, it seems."

James, who was used to thinking of himself as a very good cardplayer, was piqued by her comment. "Perhaps, after you have your meal, I will have forgotten my good manners, Madame."

She smiled widely and insincerely. "I do not believe that you have been deliberately allowing me to win—you aren't that shrewd in your bidding, for one thing." She looked around the room. "It is getting dark. How unfortunate that there are no electric lights here."

"But there are," James said impulsively, remembering Madelaine's pride at having them. "There is not enough gas to run the generator to power them. If the cars are going to be driven, it must be kerosene and candles here."

"But there is a generator? Curious." She smiled at James. "Have you seen this château when it is alight?"

"Yes," James said, not entirely sure now that he should have told her about the generator. But where was the harm, he asked himself, when a quick inspection of the old stables would reveal the generator and the allotted fuel for Montalia?

"It must be quite impressive," Madame Kunst said quietly. She was wearing one of her two dresses, an elegantly knitted creation of salmon pink with a scalloped hem and long, full sleeves. There were travel stains on the skirt and it would have been the better for cleaning and blocking. Madame Kunst fidgeted with the belt, putting her fingers through the two loops at either side of the waist. It was much more a nervous than a provocative gesture, but James could comprehend that in a lanky, high-strung way she might be attractive.

"It is," he said, taking the deck and shuffling it methodically. "After your meal, we can try again."

"Are you not going to join me?" she asked him.

"No, thank you." Then he recalled what Madelaine had said to him the first time he had dined at Montalia and he paraphrased her words. "I have a condition which severely restricts my diet. It's simpler for me to make private arrangements for my meals."

"This is the oddest household. Roger tells me that le Comte dines privately in his rooms; you have a . . . condition. If it were fitting, I would suggest to Roger that we both eat in the kitchen, but he won't hear of it." She gave a tittery laugh, then left the room.

James shuffled the cards two more times, taking time and care, then put them back in their ivory box. That done, he rose and sauntered out into the hallway, pleased to see that no one was about. Five careful minutes later, he was in Madame Kunst's room, tugging the valise from under her bed. He knelt on the floor, holding the leather case between his knees while he inspected the lock that held it closed. The valise was not unlike a large briefcase, with accordionlike sides and a metal-reenforced opening. The lock most certainly required a special key, but James thought he might be able to make some progress against it with a bent hairpin—if he could find one. He was so preoccupied that he did not hear the door open.

"You errant fool," Saint-Germain said quietly but with intense feeling.

James started up, and the valise fell heavily onto its side. "You said . . ."

"I said that you might try to draw her out when talking with her. I did not recommend you do this." He shook his head. "I might as well scribble all over the walls that we have our doubts about her. Good God, if I had wanted the lock picked, I could do that myself. Use a little *sense,* James."

James's indignation was all the greater for the disquieting suspicion that Saint-Germain was right. "I thought I was taking your hint."

"After all I told you about prudence? Truly?" He bent down and very carefully put the valise back under the bed. "If it reassures you, James, I have examined the lock already, but under less questionable circumstances. It is not as simple as it looks. Not only is there the lock you see, there is a second lock under it—and it is a good deal more complex."

"How complex?" James inquired acidly.

"It takes two keys. I am not sure why, but it does give me pause." He was already crossing the room. "We should leave. Madame Kunst sat down to her supper not long ago, but there is no reason for her to linger over the food. She may come back here shortly, and I doubt either of us could adequately explain what we are doing here."

Grudgingly, James permitted Saint-Germain to take him from the room, but as they started down the long stairs, he made one protest. "Why don't you just break into the valise and tell her that you were required to do it?"

"James, for an intelligent man, you suffer from curious lapses. Why would I do that? What excuse would she believe? And where would be the benefit?" His brows arched and he let James take whatever time he needed to answer the questions.

"Well," James said lamely as they reached the main floor again, "you would know what is in the valise."

"True enough. But do you know, I would rather find out some less compromising way." He frowned, then the frown faded. "I don't fault you for wanting the question resolved; so do I."

James accepted this with ill grace. "You aren't willing to do the obvious, so . . ."

"Do the obvious? It is not quite my style," he said sardonically. "James, play cards with the woman, listen to her, and make note of what she asks you. Tomorrow morning, I will tell her I have arranged for her transportation down the mountain, so that she can reach Nice and the boat she says she wishes to take to Scotland. That should precipitate matters."

"And what if that is what she wants—and all she wants?" James asked.

"Then Roger will do it. He has arranged with the authorities in Saint-Jacques-sur-Crete to have a travel pass when it is necessary. In these matters, the local officials are strangely flexible." He put one hand on James's arm. "Try to restrain your impulses until then, if you will. Should it turn out that we come through this with nothing more than a touch of wartime paranoia, we may count ourselves fortunate."

James had nothing to say in response, and knew that he was not very much looking forward to another round of losing at whist, but he offered no protest as he went back into the room to wait for Madame Kunst.

"Oh, thank you, Herr Comte," Madame Kunst said listlessly over a cup of weak tea the following morning.

"It was nothing, Madame. You told me that this was your wish. I only regret that it took so long to arrange the details. But surely you understand."

"Yes, of course I do." She paused to cough delicately. "I am surprised that you were able to accomplish this so quickly. After what I have been through, I expected I would have to intrude on your hospitality" (again a quiet, emphatic cough) "for a much longer time."

"It is best to act quickly in cases such as yours," Saint-Germain said ambiguously.

"How kind," she murmured, and achieved another cough.

"Is something the matter, Madame Kunst?" le Comte inquired politely, giving in.

"A slight indisposition, nothing more, I am sure." She smiled apologetically.

"Good. I would not like to think that you were ill." He rose from the chair he had taken across from her.

"Oh, I don't believe I'm that. My throat, you know. And it has been chilly." She said this last in a tone a bit more hoarse than when she had begun.

"It is often the case in the mountains," Saint-Germain said by way of courteous commiseration. "I believe there is aspirin in the château, but little else. If you like, I will ask Roger to bring you some."

Her hand fluttered up to her throat, lingered there artistically, then dropped once more. "I don't think it will be necessary. If I am troubled by it still this afternoon, then I might ask for one or two tablets."

"Very good. You may want to rest an hour or so. The drive to the coast is long and fatiguing." He left the room to the dry sound of her cough.

"She claims to be feeling poorly," Roger explained to Saint-Germain later that morning. "I brought her the tea she asked for and said that I was looking forward to taking her down to Nice. She claimed to be enthusiastic, but said she did not think she was entirely well, and did not know how easily she would travel."

"She coughed for me," Saint-Germain said. "Apparently she is not as eager as she claimed to be."

"Give her a break," James protested, watching the other two. "Maybe she's got a cold. She's been through enough."

"No matter what she has done, it's possible, of course, that she has caught a cold," Saint-Germain allowed. "But if you were as anxious as she has claimed to be to be out of this country and on your way to Scotland, would you permit a cold to keep you from completing your journey?"

"She might be worn out," James said, determined to discount anything Saint-Germain suggested. "If she's tired enough, she might not be able to fight off a cold or any other bug that happens to be around."

Saint-Germain's dark eyes were wryly amused. "Is that what you thought when you tried to search her valise? Never mind, James. We'll find out shortly what the case truly is."

"How're you planning to do that?" He was a little belligerent, and huffy.

"Why, I want to find out if she is really ill. I will offer her a remedy. If she takes it, I'll give her the benefit of the doubt. If she doesn't, then I will be extremely careful with her. As you should be." He turned away toward the old wing where he had set up his laboratory. "And James, if you would not mind, I would like to begin this myself. You may talk to her later, if you choose, but just at first, let me."

"You sound like you think I'd warn her . . ." James shot back. "I didn't get to be good at my job by shooting off my mouth."

"I am aware of that," Saint-Germain said. "But you have gallantry, my American friend, and there are those who have a way of turning that virtue to their advantage. All I ask is that you remember that."

Roger intervened before James could say anything more. "Should I get the Bugatti ready?"

"Yes. Whether Madame Kunst or one of us uses it, it doesn't matter: the car should be fueled and ready."

"You're anticipating some difficulty other than this?" James asked, looking about him involuntarily.

"Nothing specific, but in as unsettled a situation as we are in, it might be best." Saint-Germain gave James a penetrating, amused glance. "Do you wish to visit our patient in half an hour or so, to wish her godspeed?"

"Do you want me to?" James sounded irritable, but it was more from frustration at his own inactivity than genuine anger.

"Let us see how she responds to Roger." He motioned toward his manservant. "And to me."

James accepted this with a shrug and went off to the old library to pass the better part of the morning in trying to decipher the Medieval French of the oldest volumes there. He found it intriguing, and it kept him from pacing the halls like a stalking tiger.

"How are you doing, Madame Kunst?" Saint-Germain inquired of his guest as he went into her room twenty minutes after his conversation with Roger and James.

"Very well," she said listlessly.

"I trust so; the travel permit I have been able to secure for you is dated only for the next twenty-four hours. It would not be easy to get another one." He came to stand at the foot of her bed. "I can arrange for you to stop at the physician's, perhaps, but you might not wish to be subjected to the questions he is required to ask."

Madame Kunst turned blush rather than pale. "I want to keep away from officials."

"And so you shall. It is better for me, as well, to come as little to their attention as possible. Then, if it is satisfactory to you, I will make sure you have aspirin and brandy and plenty of lap rugs in the Bugatti. It will not make you entirely comfortable, but you probably will not be so until you are in Scotland." He gave her a sympathetic half-smile and watched her face.

"Yes," Madame Kunst said, her brows twitching into an expression of impatience and dissatisfaction.

Saint-Germain assumed an expression of diffidence. "My manservant has reminded me that there is another medication in the château. It is . . . an herbal remedy and very efficacious—or so I have been told. I would be pleased to bring some to you." He had made that particular elixir for more than three thousand years; it was a clear distillate that began with a solution prepared from moldy bread. The recent discovery of penicillin had amused him.

Madame Kunst looked flustered. "A peasant remedy? I don't know . . . peasants are so superstitious and some of their practices are . . . well, unpleasant."

Very gently, Saint-Germain said, "In your position, Madame Kunst, I would think you would take that chance, if only to make your ship. Brandy is a help, but you will not be clearheaded. With the herbal remedy, you need not be fuddled."

She slapped her hands down on the comforter. "But what if the remedy is worse? Some of those remedies the monks made were mostly pure spirits with a little herbal additive. This is probably more of the same thing."

"I assure you, it is not," Saint-Germain said.

"Oh, I don't know. I will have to think about it." She remembered to cough. "I have to have time to recruit my strength, Herr Comte. I will tell you in an hour or so what I have decided." With a degree of quiet malice, she added, "It was so good of you to offer this to me."

Saint-Germain bowed and left the room.

Slightly less than an hour after this, James came bursting out of Madame Kunst's room, running down the corridor, calling for Saint-Germain.

The response was almost immediate. Saint-Germain hastened from his laboratory as he tugged his lab coat off, wishing there were a way he could curb some of James's impetuosity. "A moment!" he cried as he reached the foot of the main staircase.

"We don't have a moment!" James shouted as he came into view on the upper floor. "It's urgent."

"So I gather," Saint-Germain said as he flung his wadded-up lab coat away from him. "But if it is, it might be best not to announce it to the world."

"Jesus! I forgot." He paused at the top of the stairs, then raced down them. "I don't know why it didn't occur to me. It should have."

"We will discuss it later," Saint-Germain said. "Now, what has you so up in arms?"

"Madame Kunst." He opened up his hands. "She's not in her room and her valise is gone."

"Indeed." Saint-Germain's brows rose and he nodded grimly.

"I went to her room as you instructed and it was empty. The bed was still a bit warm, so she can't have gone far or have left too long ago. If we hurry, we can find her." Now that he had forced himself to be calm, all his old journalistic habits came back. "If she's carrying that thing, she'll have to stay on the road—and that means someone will see her, if only a farmer or a shepherd."

"You're assuming she's left Montalia," Saint-Germain said. "I doubt that she has."

"Why?" James demanded.

"Because Roger is down at the gatehouse and he has not signaled me that he has seen her. Not that that makes it simpler," he added dryly. "This place is a rabbit warren and it is not easily searched."

"Especially since we don't know what we're looking for, right?" James said, running one hand through his silver hair.

"That is a factor." Saint-Germain looked up toward the ceiling. "But we also know what we are *not* looking for, which is a minor advantage." He turned away from James, his eyes on the heavy, metal-banded door to the old wing of the château. "I think she may be armed, James. Be cautious with her. Bullet wounds are painful, and if they damage the spine or skull, they are as fatal to us as to anyone else. No heroics, if you please. Madelaine would never forgive me."

James did not quite know how to take this, but he shrugged. "If that's how you want it, that's how I'll do it."

"Very good," Saint-Germain said crisply. "And we might as well begin now. First the kitchens and pantry, and then the old wing. With this precaution." He went and dropped the heavy bolt into place on the iron-banded door, effectively locking that part of the château.

"Why the kitchens first?" James asked.

"Because of the weapons it offers," Saint-Germain answered. "Knives, cleavers, forks, skewers, pokers. A kitchen is an armory on a smaller scale. If she has gone there, it will be touchy for us."

They completed their search in fifteen minutes and were

satisfied that wherever Madame Kunst was, she had not been there.

"This might not bode well. If she has panicked—which isn't likely—it is merely a matter of finding her. But if she is acting with deliberation, it means she is already prepared and we must keep that in mind."

"Does she know we're looking for her, do you think?"

"Quite possibly. That is something else to keep in mind." He was walking back toward the main hall and the barred door. "This may be somewhat more difficult. We can close off the wing, but it provides endless places to hide, to ambush."

"Great," James said with hearty sarcasm.

"Although some of the same advantages apply to us, I wish I knew what it was she is trying to do. If I did, then I could counteract it more effectively." His hand was resting on the heavy bolt.

"And you won't call the authorities," James said.

"We've had this discussion already. You know the answer. We must settle this for ourselves. And for Madelaine, since she is the one who will have to live here when this is over." He let James consider this. "You and I are transient. This is her native earth."

"Okay, okay," James said, then waved a hand at the door. "What do we do, once we get in there?"

"To begin with, we move very quietly. And we make every effort not to frighten her. Frightened people do foolish and dangerous things." He lifted the bolt and drew back the door. "For the moment, keep behind me, James. If you see or hear anything, tap my shoulder. Don't speak."

"Right," James said, feeling a bit silly. He had seen war and knew how great the risks were for those caught up in the deadly game, but skulking around the halls of an old château after a woman with a worn leather valise seemed like acting out a Grade B movie from Universal. When the door was pulled closed behind him, he was disturbed by it. The hall was very dark, with five narrow shafts of light coming from the high, notched windows. James watched Saint-Germain start toward the muniment room, and for the first time noticed the power and grace of his movements—he was controlled and feral at once, beautiful and awesome.

At the entrance to the muniment room, Saint-Germain held up

his hand to motion James to stillness. He slipped through the narrow opening, then returned several long moments later. "She is not here, but has been here," Saint-Germain told James in a whisper that was so quiet it was almost wholly inaudible. "One of the old plans of Montalia is missing."

The two rooms below the muniment room were empty and apparently untouched. James was becoming strangely nervous, as if unknown wings had brushed the back of his neck. He found it difficult to be self-contained and was all for hurrying up the search so that he could bring his restlessness back under control. "She's in the upper rooms if she's anywhere in this part of the château," James murmured, wanting to speak at a more normal level.

"Patience, James. You and I have much more time than she does." He made a last check around the small salon, then gestured to James to follow him. "We'll try the tower rooms next. Be careful of the steps."

The narrow, circular stairwell was dark at all times, but Saint-Germain carried no light. James was growing accustomed to his improved dark vision, but was still not entirely confident of this to climb without watching his feet. For once, he was the one who lagged.

The first storeroom proved empty, but Saint-Germain indicated that he wanted to make a warning trap. "Nothing complicated; a few things that will make noise if knocked over. Should she be behind us, we will have a little time," he whispered, and set about his work.

James stood on the landing, experiencing the same unpleasant sensation he had had in the lower room. On impulse, he decided to investigate the next room himself, thereby saving them time as well as giving himself the satisfaction of doing something worthwhile. He moved close to the door, as he had seen Saint-Germain do, and then opened the door just wide enough to be able to slip inside. He was dumbfounded at the sight of the valise sitting on the floor amid the other trunks and broken chairs that were stored there—and was about to call out when he sensed more than felt another presence in the room.

"Not a sound, Herr Tree," Madame Kunst said softly as she

brought up a Smith & Wesson .38 pistol. Her hands were expertly steady as she took aim at his head. "I will use this if I must."

Saint-Germain's warning flashed through James's mind—if his nervous system were damaged, if his spine or skull were broken, he would die the true death and his resurrection would have lasted merely a week—and he stood without moving. He began to dread what might happen if Saint-Germain should come into the room.

"You have been curious about the valise, haven't you? You have all been curious." She no longer looked high-strung and helpless; that part of her had been peeled away, leaving a determined woman of well-honed ruthlessness. "I have promised to see that it is left in working order—and you will not interfere." She nodded toward the valise, her aim never wavering. "Open the valise, Herr Tree."

Slowly, James did as she ordered. He dropped to his knees and pulled open the top of the old leather bag. He stared down at the contraption in it.

"It is a beacon, Herr Tree. Take it out—very, very gently—and put it on that brass trunk by the wall, the one under the window. If you trip or jolt the beacon, I will shoot you. Do you understand?"

With more care than he had ever known he possessed, James lifted the beacon. As he carried it toward the trunk she had indicated, he thought to himself that she had told him what it was, and therefore could not let him live. He put the beacon in place and hoped it was well-balanced.

"Turn around, Herr Tree," she said, softly, venomously.

James obeyed, hoping that she would not shoot in this little, narrow room. "I'm not alone."

"Herr Comte?" she asked quickly.

"Yes."

She walked up to him, just far enough to be out of reach. "And the servant?"

"I don't know," James lied, praying she would believe him. "He . . . he was told to get the car ready." He forced himself to speak in an undervoice though he wanted to shout.

"How helpful," she muttered. She glared at him, apparently wanting to make up her mind, and finally she cocked her head toward the door. "You will have to come with me, I think. You and I."

James all but ground his teeth. He wanted to rush at her, to yell so loudly that she would drop the .38 and flee from him. Neither of those things were possible, he guessed from the hint of a smile she wore. "Where are we going?" he forced himself to ask.

"Out. After that, we'll see." She was wearing her salmon-colored knit dress which in the muted light of the room looked more the shade of diseased roses. "Walk past me, Herr Tree. Hands joined behind your head." She came nearer to him. "What you feel at the base of your skull is the barrel of my pistol. If you move suddenly or try to grapple with me in any way, I will shoot. If you move your hands, I will shoot. Do I make myself clear?"

"Very."

"You will reach with your left hand—slowly and deliberately—for the door. You will open it as wide as possible and you will release it."

James did as she ordered, and when she told him to walk out onto the landing, he did that, too, as the muzzle of the .38 lay like a cold kiss on the nape of his neck.

"Now, down the stairs. One at a time. Carefully." She was speaking softly still, but the sound of her voice rang down the stones, mocking her.

On the fourth step down, James heard a sound behind him that did not come from Madame Kunst's steps. Apparently she was unaware of it, for she never faltered nor turned. He wondered if she were so confident of her mastery of the situation that she paid no attention to such things. He moved a little faster, trying to remember where the trip stair was.

"Not so fast," Madame Kunst insisted. "It's dark in here."

Obediently, James slowed. He heard the whisper-light tread behind her, and wished he dared to turn. The trip stair was only a few treads below him. He made his way carefully.

Then, just as he passed the trip stair, something tremendously strong swept by him on the narrow, curving stair, knocking him to the side and catching Madame Kunst on the most unstable footing in the tower.

She screamed, twisted. She fired once, twice, and the bullets ricocheted off the stone walls, singeing and striking sparks where they touched. One of the bullets struck her in the shoulder and she fell, then slid downward, screaming at first and then whimpering. Her descent stopped only when Saint-Germain reached her.

"You may get up, James," he said as he lifted Madame Kunst into his arms.

Moving as if he were tenanted in a body that was unfamiliar to him, James rose, testing his legs like an invalid. When he was shakily on his feet again, he looked down at the other man. "Thank you."

"Thank *you*, James. Your methods were reckless, but your motive laudable." He looked down at Madame Kunst, who was half-conscious and moaning. "I should bandage her and get her to a physician. There must be a plausible story we can tell him."

James had not the strength to laugh at this as he came down the stairs.

"But it will arrange itself," Mirelle said confidently with a nonchalant French shrug. "A refugee woman, she says, came to my farmhouse—and I, what could I do but take her in? I did not know that she was carrying valuables and, when there was a commotion, I investigated." Her minx's eyes danced as she looked up at James. "It was very nice of you to give me the pistol, Mister Tree. I would not have been able to defend her if you had not been so generous." She held out her hand for the pistol.

"How do you explain the rest? The beacon and her wound?" Saint-Germain asked, not quite smiling, but with the corners of his mouth starting to lift.

Mirelle gave this her consideration. "I don't think I will explain the beacon. I think I will present it to a few of my friends in the Resistance and they will see what kind of game it attracts. For the rest, the thief was holding Madame . . . Kunst, isn't it? . . . so tightly that I was not in a position to get a clean shot." She sat back in the high-backed chair that was the best in her parlor. "The physician in Saint-Jacques-sur-Crete will not ask me too many questions because he likes me and he hates the Germans and the war. Beyond that—who knows? The Germans may take her back; the Resistance may kill her. It does not matter so much, does it?" She folded her hands.

"Mirelle," Saint-Germain said, with more sadness than she had ever heard in his voice, "you cannot simply abandon her like so much refuse."

"You say that—after she tried to kill James and would have killed you?" Mirelle shot back at him. "You defend her?"

"Yes," was the quiet answer.

Mirelle got out of her chair and turned her helpless eyes on James, then looked away from them both. "Perhaps you can afford to feel this way, you who live so long and so closely with others. But I am not going to live that long, and I have very few years to do all that I must. Extend her your charity, if you must, but do not expect it of me. My time is too brief for that." She folded her arms and stared defiantly at Saint-Germain.

"You have chosen it," Saint-Germain reminded her compassionately; he took her hand and kissed it.

"So I have," she agreed with her impish smile returning. "For the time, I have the best of both, and when that is done, well, we shall see." She turned toward James. "Would you like to remain here for the evening, James?"

"Thank you, Mirelle, but no." He glanced out the window to the parked Bugatti.

"Another time, then. I will be at Montalia tomorrow night?" Her eyes went flirtatiously from Saint-Germain's to James's face. "You would like that, yes?"

"Of course," Saint-Germain said, answering for James.

"Then, good afternoon, gentlemen, and I will see you later. I have a few old friends who will want to hear from me—and the physician to mollify." Without any lack of courtesy, she escorted them to the door and stood waving as the Bugatti pulled away.

James returned the wave, then looked at Saint-Germain. "What *will* happen to Madame Kunst?"

"I don't know," he said quietly.

"Does it concern you at all?" James was beginning to feel a twinge of guilt.

"Yes. But it is out of my hands now." He drove in silence.

M44

"Just that easy, is it?" James demanded some minutes later when he had been alone with his thoughts.

Saint-Germain's small hands tightened on the steering wheel. "No, James—and it never becomes easy."